Crisis in the Congo

James Bell

ISBN-13: 987-1500519612

ISBN-10: 1500519618

CRISIS IN THE CONGO

Dedication

To Heidi, my wife, my muse, my toughest critic and companion for most of my life.

Foreward

This is a work of historical fiction that takes place in the Republic of Congo between October 1959 and September 1961 during its transition to independence. It is based on true events and characters in that period, though there are fictitious figures included in the story.

I've tried to recount this remarkable time based on research into publicly available historical documents, prior works of non-fiction and my own imagination. I hope I have cast the real characters in an accurate light, although there are numerous liberties taken with the narrative for dramatic effect.

Fifty-five years later, this period and place in world history is largely unknown or forgotten. The genesis of the idea for writing this book came from an article I read in the July/August 2014 *Foreign Affairs* magazine, entitled 'What Really Happened. Solving the Cold War's Cold Cases: Congo 1961.' What I found out reinforced the old adage that truth is stranger than any fictitious account I might be able to create.

Another part of my inspiration came from my uncle, Lucien Irving 'Stag' Thomas, a highly decorated tailgunner who fought in World War II, the Korean War and the Viet Nam War. He concluded his career working in an ill-defined and vaguely discussed position for a mining company in South Africa and Angola in the 1970s.

This is my fourth book, but the first attempt to take on the genre of historical fiction. Researching the characters and events in this period has been the most rewarding part of the process. Most of the Congolese were larger-than-life characters who lived in a wildly unpredictable era that none of them could have imagined in 1959. They were defined by a brutal colonial history in an enormous, still untamed country in the center of Africa. I only hope that I have brought the history and people faithfully to life.

James Bell

March 2015

The Central Characters

(in order of appearance)

Richard Penderel	U.S. Consulate Officer, Congo
George Denman	U.S. Chief of Station, Congo
Clare Timberlake	U.S. Consular General, later U.S. Ambassador to Congo
Rene Delvaux	Export Director, Société Générale de Belgique
Beryl Reader	Geology Professor, University of Elisabethville
Jean-Pierre Biver	Chairman, Union Minière du Haut Katanga
Timothy Reader	Commercial Relations Officer, Northern Rhodesia
Moise Tshombe	President, Province of Katanga
Leon Tucci	Deputy Chief of Station, Congo

The Central Characters

(in order of appearance)

Habib Khouri	Owner, Le Restaurant Cedars Élevé, U.S. Operative
Harold d'Aspremont	Belgian Minister for African Affairs
Justin-Marie Bomboko	Foreign Affairs Minister, Congo
Victor Nendaka	Head of Security Services, Congo
Prescott Dillon	Chief of Africa Division, CIA
Patrice Lumumba	Prime Minister, Congo
Joseph Kasavubu	President, Congo
Joseph Mobutu	Army Chief of Staff, Congo
Cyrille Adoula	Prime Minister, Congo
Dag Hammarskjöld	U.N. Secretary-General

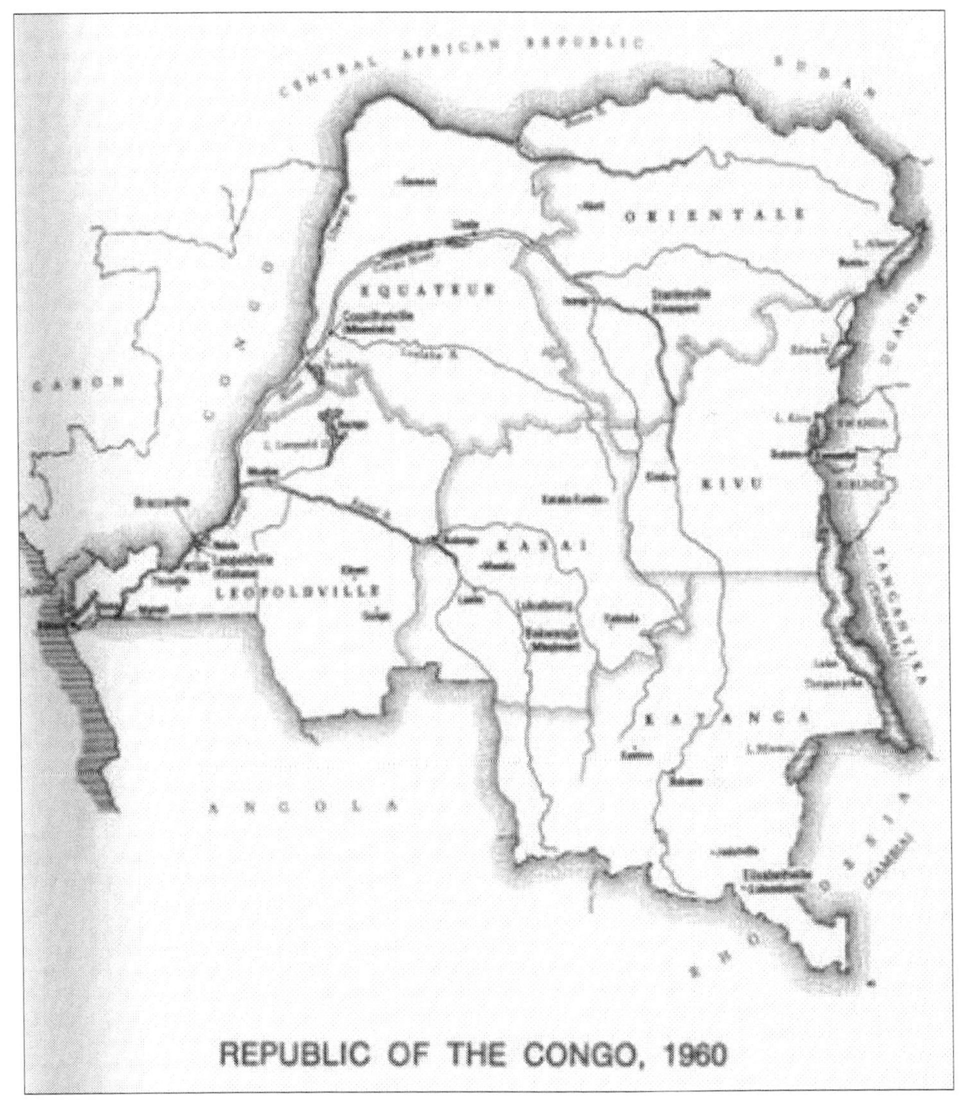

REPUBLIC OF THE CONGO, 1960

One

November 1959

The Sabena Douglas DC-7C droned in and out of the massive rain clouds hiding the rising sun. Dicky Penderel glanced out of the porthole, checked his watch and lit a cigarette. It was 6:15. One more hour to go. The flight had been endless. The sky was murky and leaden. He inhaled cigarette smoke and leaned against the plexiglas, gazing at the landscape below. He could already feel the humidity seeping through the seal of the porthole. Small fires on the ground gave depth to the soupy vista and to the brooding green carpet of jungle that went on and on, clear to the horizon.

His knees ached. It was no doubt due to way too many missions kneeling in the tiny rear turrets of Lancaster bombers firing Browning machine guns at German Messerschmitts over northern Europe. At least this Douglas was civilized aviation. No one was shooting at you. Penderel took another drag on the cigarette and looked about the front cabin. It was nearly empty.

Across the aisle, a portly black man, face shining, sat straight up in his seat, splayed chin resting on his jowls. He had on a dark suit, white button down shirt and a skinny repp tie that appeared to be strangling him. He looked like a bullfrog, still and breathing rhythmically. A thin European sat in front of Penderel, but politely he hadn't put his seat back during the flight. The man had read all through the night. His light was an irritant when Penderel stirred and tried to get comfortable.

'Voulez-vous un café? Nous allons atterrir à Léopoldville en 30 minutes,' the cheerful blond stewardess asked. Penderel wondered how she could look so fresh. Her blond hair was pulled back in a bun under a stylish pillbox navy hat. Her uniform was tailored, drawn in at the waist and she had beautiful long hands with red nails. She had turned her head to the side, both flirtatious and polite, when she asked him if he cared for coffee. He felt greasy and disoriented and stank of the cigarettes and whiskey he'd consumed during the night. He couldn't wait for the hotel room and a long, hot shower.

'That would be terrific. I'd like it black, no sugar.'

'Je vous en prie,' she answered, walking briskly back to the galley. Penderel stubbed out his cigarette and watched her disappear behind the curtain. He looked out of the window again.

The shacks sitting on muddy roads carved out of the pregnant landscape became more plentiful and visible as the plane banked for the initial landing approach. Penderel could make out rusty tin corrugated roofs and a few brightly painted signs, as the plane roared through the morning silence. Reflections sparkled off the thick chocolate milk capillaries of the great Congo River -- the skeleton for this enormous landmass. It was languid and shrouded, he thought, capable of hiding many things.

'Merci,' Penderel replied, as she returned with a tray and the cup and saucer. The lengthy flights from the U.S. had made him tired, hung over and horny. He had plenty of time for fantasies and took full advantage of his solitariness to indulge in them. He had better get used to it – a white forty-year-old posted to a colonial black country. It was his first posting abroad, this lumbering backwater in the dead center of Africa. It was rumored to be cozy.

'There lots of black tie dinners. Take two dinner jackets, as the cleaners aren't always prompt. And bring your golf clubs,' the agent told him stateside.

The briefings had been helpful, but they were just words on pages of paper, written in a terse government, acronym-laden argot that kept the narrative in outline form. He wasn't a policy guy, or much of a student of post-colonial governance. He couldn't wait to feel the stickiness and understand the backstory. Things came into focus for him through experience.

‚ians had promoted a thirty-year path toward .ce, but the plan was rejected. There were isola.. ›ts in Léopoldville, Stanleyville, and a few of the larger cities throughout the year. A few political parties had been formed, but there wasn't any momentum. The country was too large and disconnected to have a meaningful national election. The Belgian Congo would be better off as part of a loose federation, so long as the U.S. controlled the mines in the southeast. The expats were increasingly nervous. He'd been briefed on all of the scenarios. Between the lines, it seemed that this process wasn't going to end well.

The pilot came over the PA system. Penderel listened carefully. His French was passable, though he knew it needed to get a lot better. The cram course helped, but he was still far more comfortable reading than hearing it. Then the pilot repeated the announcement, 'Ladies and Gentlemen, we are approaching N'djili airport in Léopoldville. We will be landing in fifteen minutes. The temperature upon arrival will be 74 degrees Fahrenheit rising to a high of 88 degrees by afternoon. It has been a pleasure to serve you on Sabena World Airlines.'

Penderel checked his dossier, excited by what was ahead. He had never been to Africa, except for a few days in Cairo after the war. This was the real Africa, the heart of darkness, the land of Livingstone and Stanley.

'Do you have anything to declare?' the uniformed official asked as Penderel presented his passport and papers.

'No, I'm with the U.S. Consulate,' he volunteered, cheerfully. The customs agent thumbed through the passport without speaking.

'I will still need to look through your suitcase.' The agent unzipped Penderel's large leather case and absentmindedly picked through his belongings. He opened the toiletries bag quickly, fiddled through it and reclosed it. He smiled as he picked up the carton of 555 cigarettes that were in a handbag. 'Good tobacco.' he smiled, returning them carefully to their place in the bag.

'Yes, would you care for one?' Penderel had been forewarned to pack light, except for cigarettes. It was the common currency for getting anything done.

'Oui, Monsieur,' he answered cheerfully, looking birdlike around the customs hall.

'Here. Please take a pack.'

'Welcome to the Belgian Congo, sir. I hope you enjoy your stay.'

A small man with large black-framed glasses stood outside the immigration hall with a neatly printed sign 'RICHARD PENDEREL, ESQ.' He had on a white dress shirt with a black glasses holder in his top pocket.

'Monsieur Penderel? I'm Antoine, your driver.'

'Good to meet you. Please call me Dicky.'

'Yes, Monsieur Dicky,' Antoine laughed, catching himself. 'Welcome to Léopoldville. How was your flight?'

'Long,' Penderel answered. 'And boring. I couldn't sleep.'

'Well, Monsieur, we will get you to The Memling *toute de suite*. A hot shower will do the trick,' Antoine answered, leading the way to the car. The heat and humidity hit Penderel like a moving wall. A strong smell of rotten vegetation arose from the sickly grass growing out of the cracked, grey concrete walkway. The sun peeked through a bank of gathering clouds, giving the morning an eerie translucence. The French signs 'ARRIVÉE' and 'PARC DE STATIONNEMENT' gave him a rush of adrenalin – the welcome mat of a new and unfamiliar place. Still he felt like shit. His head throbbed and his ears were ringing as they approached the car. He was dripping wet.

'Under further consideration,' Penderel thought to himself. 'Maybe a cold shower would be better.' He slid his lanky frame across the back seat, rolled down the window and lit a cigarette. The breeze blowing in through the back window of the 1957 white Renault Dauphine was refreshing. He'd heard Léopoldville was going to be the city of the future.

The riots earlier in the year paralyzed the city and awoke the Eisenhower administration. Otherwise he'd still be back at Langley, learning this new trade. Independence fever was sweeping through Africa, yet America remained on the periphery of influence. This was still Europe's continent. Up to now, the U.S. could preach about freedom and democracy for all and not worry about the consequences. But now, the U.S. was being thrust into the middle of changing events it wasn't prepared for.

His superior officer back in the States repeatedly told him that global leadership required hypocrisy. The cynicism of the comment chapped Penderel. He generally saw things in black and white terms, where you did what you said. Nuance and indirection were still things he was learning in order to be a 'consular officer.'

By the look of the view outside the car window, everything seemed to be in limbo. It surely didn't appear to be the future of urban development. More like the last gasp of a second-rate empire trying to make a statement. Big slabs of ugly and unassembled concrete block sat along the wide Boulevard Albert 1er. The Parliament building was nearing completion, though it looked to Penderel that it still had a long way to go. Several other buildings were under construction as well, rebar and open bags of cement strewn along the roadway, unattended.

This was never going to be Brussels in the jungle, though he knew the country possessed the resources to become a continental power. He read in the dossier that there were enough uranium, copper, cobalt and diamonds in the ground that this country should be able to be stable, if not prosperous. It was so much to take in. He realized he had little time to make sense of it. But it was a helluva lot better than those endless briefing books and unintelligible codenames.

The traffic stopped. There was instantaneous honking. Then a peal of sirens rang out of the still morning heat. 'Oh no,' Antoine said. 'This might be awhile.'

'What's the holdup?' asked Penderel anxiously. The sleepy traffic had knotted up and the sirens got louder.

'Protests,' Antoine replied. 'Every day there is something. Mostly they are peaceful. Earlier this year, it got out of hand. Hundreds were killed.' He rattled his thumbs against the steering wheel, shaking his head. 'Traffic didn't used to be like this.' He seemed more blasé and impatient than anxious or angry.

'Why now?' Penderel was sweating, now the car had stopped. 'Pro-Independence?'

'Yes, probably. A few times it has been government workers wanting better pay. But mostly it's about elections. The Belgians keep promising us a voice, but nothing ever happens. Hope you Americans can help us.'

Gat-gat-gat-gat. Rat-at-at-at-at. Dakka-dakka.

'What in the hell is that? That sounds like gunfire.' Penderel looked out of the window. There was yelling and smoke on the sidewalk thirty yards ahead. He couldn't see anything. 'What's going on?' he shouted.

'Keep your head down, Monsieur,' answered Antoine, trying to turn the car around on the densely packed main boulevard. Horns carried over the gunfire. *Gat-gat-gat-gat. Dakka-dakka-dakka.*

Antoine wheeled the Renault up on the sidewalk, knocking over a large trashcan. Penderel peeked out of the right rear window, keeping his head down as instructed, while Antoine noisily shifted gears in reverse. Two shopkeepers had rushed out onto the street to see what was going on. The stench of tear gas stung his eyes and he rolled the window shut.

Up ahead, several people lay along the roadway, bloody and still. Several others were throwing rocks and small metal cans into the smoke. *Rat-at-at-at-at. Rat-at-at-at-at.* Just then a loud bass *boom-boom-boom* echoed through the wide, canyoned roadway.

'Force Publique, sir,' Antoine injected. 'Must be a big riot.' Penderel could make out four black soldiers dressed in tightly tailored, blue uniforms with white pantaloons and red fezes stabbing bayonets wildly into the acrid smoke. Just then, a group of barefoot men carrying automatic rifles ran by the car screaming. Two had their rifles slung on their shoulders and were carrying a bloody body. A small man ran behind wild-eyed and shrieking, carrying a man twice his size on his back. The man being carried appeared to have part of his skull severed. Three other men sprinted by the car, one handspringing over the bonnet and disappearing down a side street.

Antoine had finally turned the car around and it screeched as he sped along the sidewalk, knocking over two small makeshift tented shops and flattening canvas spreads of food and bicycle innertubes. 'Sorry sir,' he yelled out the window as they rammed a small motorcycle chained to a signpost, before turning onto Avenue Des Flamboyants, then a quick left onto Avenue Prince de Liege. They sped along as ambulances and a M8 Greyhound armored car headed toward the scene of the protest.

Penderel could still hear the gunfire, but it was increasingly muffled.

'We look to be safe now. Is this over?' Penderel asked, breathless.

'Yes, Monsieur, we are safe.'

'Is this common? Lots of people were probably killed back there. Ten? Fifteen maybe?'

'Maybe. Maybe more. Hard to tell. It's not so common, Monsieur. But more frequent. It happens maybe once a week. It's worse at night.'

Penderel chuckled, sitting back in the rear seat, dazed at the sudden violence. 'They told me to bring two dinner jackets, not a Browning M1919,' he snickered to himself. The briefings had referred to 'occasional civil unrest in the large cities,' but not a pitched battle in the center of the city on an otherwise quiet Tuesday morning.

'Antoine, care for a cigarette?' Penderel asked, catching his breath. They turned right onto the main roadway. The Boulevard Albert 1er regained a sense of normalcy, as they headed east away from the riot. 'Think I need to settle my nerves before I meet Mr. Denman.'

Antoine looked into the rear mirror and responded with a quick smile. 'Oui, Monsieur.'

They slowly inhaled the strong, blue smoke, enjoying the deep breath and slight dizziness as Antoine turned onto the Avenue Bas-Congo. The sweet smell from a stand of gardenias wafted through the car windows and it immediately took Penderel to the exotic, tranquil place he had been briefed on. The morning had finally slowed down.

'Monsieur Dicky, we are nearing the hotel,' said Antoine, pointing to the seven-story hotel overlooking the street. 'Monsieur Denman wants to meet you at 1 p.m. for lunch. Is that acceptable, sir?'

'Yes, that would be perfect. Thank you, Antoine. You handled that situation back there very well. I look forward to working with you.'

Two

The Chief of Station cut a confident swath as he strode across the patio to the outdoor table at Le Pergola. He was small, thin, non-descript man, easily lost in a different place. He was exhaling the remains of a cigarette as he approached the table. 'Good afternoon,' he said, sticking out his hand. 'Welcome to Léopoldville. I'm George Denman. Nice to finally meet you in person. You must be unnerved after that testy drive into town. I apologize for such a rude introduction.'

'Hi, Richard Penderel. It's nice to finally meet you too,' he replied, grasping Denman's firm hand. 'The gunfight was quite a surprise. Is it common?'

'Increasingly so, unfortunately,' Denman answered. 'Not something we tend to advertise to our new visitors. But it's been building over the past year and will get worse.'

Penderel smiled at the deadpan answer and noticed Denman's sharp, darting blue eyes. They were alert, yet unemotional. They'd seen this kind of stuff before.

'How was your flight?' asked Denman.

'I'm a little fuzzy, but I feel OK. At least the stewardess was pretty.'

'Yes, they are a nice distraction. Could I get you a cocktail?' Denman asked. 'I recommend something with quinine.'

'That would be perfect,' said Penderel. *A drink would certainly calm my nerves.*

'Sabena has been flying that route from Brussels since 1925,' Denman continued, lighting another cigarette. 'The first flight took 51 days. Didn't Phileas Fogg go around the world in eighty days? Now they have DC-7s. I understand you know a bit about planes?'

'A bit,' Penderel answered, smiling. 'I was better at shooting at them than flying them. But a lot has changed since I was last in the sky. Seems things on the ground have gotten more complicated.'

'That's why you're here and here sooner than originally planned,' Denman answered, with a quick smile. 'And things are *very* complicated. You saw a bit of it today. And you'll see more soon, I'm afraid. But for now, let's toast to the simple things we can control – to gin, quinine and success ahead.'

Penderel's new boss had a reputation as a workaholic. George Denman spoke several languages and reportedly had a sharp mind and little tolerance for inaction. He started with the OSS at the outbreak of the war. He'd been posted to Istanbul and London, then Brussels until early this year, when he was named Chief of Station for the Belgian Congo.

'I'm still trying to get the lay of the land. Langley completely relied on the Belgians,' Denman began as two plates of sautéed fish arrived at the table. 'I've been here not quite a year and it's still a puzzle. The Belgians clearly don't know what the fuck is going on. Stupid arrogant people! They don't realize that the colonial era is over. We need to jump in or the fucking Soviets will.' Denman was talking and purposefully shoveling food. His rise in aggravation coincided with his eating pace.

'We need to get you down to Katanga next week to meet Biver,' Denman continued. 'He's a piece of work. Nice smart man. Belgian engineer running a company that makes up half of the government's revenues. It's another world in Elisabethville. The more you peel away, the bigger and more rotten this big piece of fruit is.' He exhaled and took a sip of his drink and another bite of fish.

'So I'm beginning to observe.'

Penderel walked next door, climbed the flight of stairs and returned to his room. The air conditioner was loud and rattling. The condensation on the window obscured his first lengthy view of the new boulevard under construction. The room was dark and a dingy, a discolored mosquito net hung over the four-poster bed.

He lay down on the bed and took his shoes off. He was exhausted, but couldn't turn his mind off. The staccato memory of the wild-eyed, barefoot man gurgling and screaming with a hacked-up body over his shoulder kept pulsing. Instantaneous violence. He'd experienced war, but at a distance, mostly far above the fight. The skies over Europe and Korea weren't safe, but they were far less graphic. He'd never experienced street-to-street, hand-to-hand combat. *'And bring your golf clubs.'* Jesus fucking Christ! Somebody has a sense of humor.

His six-foot-three frame hung over the end of the bed, but he didn't care. His thinning blond hair was damp and he thought his bright red, heat-stroked face was going to explode. But the darkened room, mosquito net and clattering window unit made him feel protected. Outside of that, he wasn't sure. Today, he'd just get his bearings and some sleep. Tomorrow, work started.

Denman returned to the consulate and read through several cables that had come in over lunch. The mission was small and unremarkable, sitting on a quiet side street surrounded by ill-kempt vegetation. There were thirteen people working there, including consul general, Clare 'Tim' Timberlake, a thirty-year Foreign Service veteran. For the past year, Timberlake had warned his superiors at the State Department that a violent uprising was likely.

Denman decided to phone his Belgian counterpart, Rene Delvaux. 'What kind of shit is going on?' he shouted into the receiver. 'My new man in town almost got his ass shot off in the crossfire. Can't you get your goddamned army from starting a firefight ten blocks from the consulate? Who was the stupid son-of-a-bitch in charge of those idiots?'

'Calm down, my friend, calm down. It was a mistake. We will keep this stuff out of the city.'

'Yeah, yeah, yeah. Keep talking. Word has it that several of the protesters were carrying Kalishnikovs. Please tell me how a bunch of poor, uneducated, unemployed natives get a hold of Russian automatic rifles.' Denman took a deep breath as he shifted the phone to his other ear.

'George, we don't know, but it's not the first time we've encountered them. Several of the protesters from riots up in Stanleyville last month had them, too. The Soviets have an arms pipeline. We just can't find it.'

'Goddamn it, Rene. If you can't adequately police this country, we will. The last thing any of us need right now is any more trouble than we already have. Either you ensure there's law and order, or we will find a way to achieve that. Am I being clear?'

'As always, delicately so,' answered Delvaux with a snicker. 'By the way, how's the new boy? He's the flyboy hero, right?'

'We'll see. I couldn't blame him for turning around and getting on the next plane out of this hellhole,' snarled Denman, tamping his cigarette out three forceful times in the overflowing ashtray. 'So far as I can tell, he has a sex drive and likes a drink. Be on the lookout for him. I think you'll get along fine. Au-revoir, Rene.'

'I will, George. And again, I'm sorry this happened. I'll call General Janssens right away.'

The Belgians had not prepared its colony for any form of independence. There were fewer than twenty college graduates out of a population of fourteen million. No doctors, dentists, architects, university professors, lawyers or accountants. The officer corps of the national army, the *Force Publique,* was exclusively white and Belgian.

Denman and Timberlake had observed a slow grinding war for independence in Algeria, where nearly a million people had died over the past five years. They watched Ghana gain independence in 1957, then Guinea last year. The 'winds of change,' as British Prime Minister Harold MacMillan put it, were blowing derecho-like through the African continent.

And Belgian Congo, a continental-sized country in the center, was not ready to go it alone. To begin with, they didn't have the right teachers. What was Belgium? A tiny, divided doormat to invaders in Northern Europe that couldn't decide whether to align with France or Holland.

But the real story was the minerals. Specifically, uranium and cobalt. Since the 1920s, Belgian Congo had a virtual monopoly of the world uranium market. Belgium's mining giant, the Union Minière du Haut Katanga, had supplied the U.S. with 1,500 tons of uranium to build the first atomic bombs that were dropped on Japan in 1945. Geologists working for the Atomic Energy Commission described it as a 'tremendously rich lode of uranium pitchblende.' In a time when the AEC considered ore containing .003 a 'good find,' this ore was 65 percent pure uranium.

That was something that the Soviet Union was also all too aware of.

Three

Late November 1959

'So you're the new *consul* in town?' Rene Delvaux asked Penderel with a wink. Delvaux was a tall man with a mop of wavy gray hair and a close-cropped beard. He wore small gold-rimmed glasses, which made him look more like an artist than a representative of the Kingdom of Belgium.

When they took their seats, Penderel noticed Delvaux cross his long, thin legs and tuck one foot behind the other leg. He looked to be a human form of a caduceus, legs intertwined with proud moving wings as he talked and gestured. Like Penderel, Delvaux had a title that didn't quite match his responsibilities with his embassy. The title on his business card was 'Export Director' for some bank in Belgium. 'Where are you staying now?'

'Just moved into a flat near the consulate,' Penderel answered. 'It's pretty basic, but closeby. I've been working a lot getting up to speed. This is my one respite – a drink and a bowl of noodles. Glamorous life.'

'Do you play tennis?' Delvaux asked. 'Some weekend I'll have you to the club to meet a few people. Mostly Belgians. But a nice escape from the world of diplomacy.'

'That would be nice. I'd like that. I'd been told to bring my golf clubs, but I enjoy tennis, too,' he answered. 'Any single ladies about?'

Delvaux laughed out loud, clutching his whiskey. 'Ah, you Americans work too hard! There are a few brave women around. But most of them are married. Not happily so, mind you, nor are they particularly faithful. Happy to make some introductions.' He flashed a knowing grin.

'My wife and three children live in Leuven. Not worth the trouble to uproot them at this point. I go back six times a year. It seems to be enough for all of us.'

'Do you know Moise Tshombe?' Penderel asked.

'He's a friend of Belgium's … and of yours, by the way. You'll learn that,' he sighed, breathing out a choreographed set of smoke rings. 'With all the political uproar, he's a steady ally. But you already know that.'

'Yes, that's what I've heard,' Penderel answered. 'I'm supposed to meet him soon.'

'He's one of the good ones here who gets it. The rest of these people are stupid and parochial. When independence happens – and it will sometime soon – this place will disintegrate. It'll split into four countries. A lot of people will get killed. God only knows about this Lumumba character!'

'He's quite the politician,' Penderel replied. 'What's your assessment?'

'That's just it. He is a politician -- all charisma, no practical sense. He'll drive this place into a ditch. You mark my words.' He paused to note Penderel's expression, before continuing. 'He's all about pan-Africanism, power to the masses, screw the colonials. That's his patter -- like a 78 on a broken Victrola. If Belgium hadn't colonized this place, they'd still be running around throwing spears at each other.'

'You're probably right,' Penderel replied, not liking the coarse caricature or the rosy recollection of Belgium's atrocious colonial history. 'How long will it take for this place to stand on its own two feet?'

'Thirty years? A hundred years? Probably never! They are children with adult resources. Want some candy, little boy? How about four million francs for some copper and cobalt? That is the crux of the problem. And why you Yanks are coming in now.'

Penderel smiled. In many ways, he was dead right, but independence was inevitable and a steady supply of minerals headed to the U.S. was non-negotiable. 'Yes, my friend,' he replied. 'I fully understand what you are talking about. We share similar perspectives.

'I have a meeting with Jean-Pierre Biver next week in Elisabethville,' he continued. 'Any thing I should know?'

Delvaux had relaxed since his rant. He sat back in the wicker chair and lit another cigarette, motioning for a glass of sherry. 'Well, I expect you've been briefed. He's looking forward to discussing business with you.'

Rene Delvaux was an old Africa hand. Born to a wealthy Belgian family who owned the Brasserie Piedboeuf in Jupille-sur-Meuse, Delvaux spent his years up until the war in country houses and restaurants all over the continent. Quick-witted and kind, he was a gifted conversationalist and raconteur with the ability to tell anecdotes in German, French, Dutch and English. He joined the Sûreté de l'État in 1936 and moved to London four years later with the government in exile.

After the war, he moved back to Belgium with his young family for a management job within the service, helping to organize the internal procedures for better tracking Soviet agents and spies.

But the desk job that consisted of little more than writing rules and procedures bored the about-to-be-forty father of two, as did the droning life in a grey, bombed-out, still-anxious city which had put up no resistance to the Nazi invasion. Brussels was a proud, yet brittle city, whose citizens still put on their fine woolen blazers before heading out to scrounge for fresh food and heating oil.

Delvaux wanted something more, something different; something that could rekindle his love of adventure. An old friend Edgar Sengier, a director for Société Générale de Belgique, a large banking organization that had advised his family's beer business for generations, suggested the Belgian Congo. Sengier had been the director for the UMHK during the War and had been the go-between for the Manhattan Project.

In 1952, Rene Delvaux arrived in Léopoldville as an export director for Société Générale. He brought joie de vivre, five dinner jackets, a small Rene Magritte and a comprehensive knowledge of Belgium's mining interests in its one and only colony.

Penderel returned to the consulate and briefed Denman on the conversation.

'Not surprising,' Denman smiled. 'Rene's a soldier like us. Sûreté de l'État, though you won't hear that from him. He always has his country's best interests at heart. He's politically wired, comes from aristocracy, though he's not the usual stuffy Belgian. A good person, but be wary. The Belgians are only interested in money and maintaining control of the mines. The rest of the country is lost. This is their Alamo.'

'When do I get introduced to Tshombe?'

'Not this trip,' Denman answered. 'We'll need a little more lead time for that. He'd be insulted to be contacted at the last minute for a meeting. A very regal guy, believe he's a king of some sort. But he has his own agenda about what happens. As the picture gets more detailed up close, you'll see more from a distance.'

'Like Seurat?' Penderel muttered.

'An art history buff, eh?' Denman laughed. 'Didn't you drop out of some fancy boarding school and join the Canadian RAF in '39 to fight for the Brits?'

Penderel smiled. 'I was full of youthful exuberance for the Commonwealth. My mother was Kenyan. Thought we were all Allies against the Nazis.'

'Well, FDR took his sweet time getting in. Hard to believe that was twenty years ago,' Denman said, lighting a cigarette. His drab office was cramped, files strewn around the floor. The air conditioner rattled. Denman slept on a mangy green sofa a few nights a week. Judging by the indentations, he'd likely been there last night. There was nothing suave about the Chief of Station.

'This enemy now is shrewder and just as lethal,' he continued. 'After all, they're the best chess players on earth. But, like us, the Russians are still feeling their way around. Doubt they could pull off a Hungary or a Poland here. Still, they know where the prize is.'

'Yes, I understand. Anything in particular I should be listening for?'

'No, this is a social trip for you to meet the most powerful man in Belgian Congo and probably our strongest ally. Straight shooter. He's an engineer by training. Katanga is their fortress. A lot of stuff goes on there that we'd like to know about, but keep our distance from. It's better that way.'

Penderel turned to Denman. He was sitting on the edge of his desk, sleeves rolled up, tie loosened, still smoking, short hair oily and matted. His black browline glasses were perched akilter on his head. He was not a man who looked into the mirror much. 'The briefings say that Biver and Tshombe maintain a private army in addition to the Katanga gendarmerie. Is that true?'

'Probably, but we don't need to pry too much into that. Whatever best protects our mutual interests. Dicky, you'll learn that much goes on here that you don't see. A silent hand. They say that about the river here too. It controls everything.'

Penderel walked back to his new flat. It was Spartan, consisting of one bedroom, a small kitchenette and a sitting area with minimal décor and mismatched colors. He was a bachelor, who had spent a good deal of his life moving around, collecting stories, memories and medals, but little in the way of possessions.

He suspected it came from a picaresque, but lonely childhood. His American father, Donald Penderel, had joined Standard Oil in Amoy in 1900 and was rumored to be the model for the protagonist in the popular novel, *Oil for the Lamps of China.* His Nairobi-born mother Helen was attending a boarding school in England when she met the dashing young oilman nearly twice her age. They married quickly in 1920.

Richard McKenzie Penderel was born in Bournemouth, England in 1921 and moved to Richmond, Virginia in 1925. He led a privileged but lonely life, with a traveling father and a young mother who drank until she died at 34, a casualty of verbal and psychological torment over her short, tortured marriage. There were platoons of nannies and servants, who became his close friends in the enormous, empty house on Cary Street Road. At eighteen, he ran away from boarding school in Connecticut, bought a first-class train ticket to Montreal and joined the Royal Canadian Air Force.

He was excited about the trip to Elisabethville in the morning and it would be his first plane ride since arriving a month earlier. He'd read about all of these characters and Denman had briefed him about what to say.

But what he looked forward to the most was getting out of Léopoldville and seeing what this enormous place looked like. His existence over the first four weeks consisted of working ten hours a day at the consulate, punctuated by meals and a hundred-yard walk to and from his flat. He wasn't sure how he felt about a desk job. It was so constricting and monotonous. But he wasn't a kid anymore and his body couldn't take the physical toll of combat flying – even if there was a war he could be posted to. Tomorrow will be a needed break in routine and a chance to get back in the sky, he thought to himself.

So far, he liked Denman well enough. Not much personality, all business, but so were most of his superiors in the air force. Timberlake seemed like a decent sort – a genteel state department guy with a quick smile and a practical mind. But there was so much talking and hashing out the same issues over and over again -- Belgium, independence, the uranium, the Soviets. Tomorrow he was going to finally experience it firsthand.

Four

Early December 1959

The 600-mile Sabena flight to Elisabethville took five hours. The view outside the window was monotonous – mile after mile of the same steamy green vista, punctuated by brown rivers and rolling waves of thick, grey clouds. As a former airman, he looked for clearings in case of emergencies, but none were obvious. *If we go down here, no one will ever find us.* He thought back to that forced bailout over the Yellow Sea seven years earlier. He jerked from his dozing, as he remembered paddling around in the water, waiting for the recon plane to spot them. He shook his head quickly, a quick jerk as if to fling the memory from his thoughts.

Penderel's mind turned to the practical realities of independence and challenges of governing a country this enormous. How could anyone get a grip on someplace as vast and disconnected? The Russians have the same damn problem. They've tried for forty years to build a cohesive country out of an unwieldy landmass and it hasn't worked yet. Probably never will. It has to be held together by force. Same as this place.

A silent hand. Sounded like melodramatic spy talk, but Denman seemed to be a realist, not a poet. Penderel liked his intensity, focus and profanity. But there was an irritating vagueness to him that he guessed came with the occupational territory.

The flight was full of white Europeans and a few pumped-up, well-dressed Congolese men who ran the white stewardess ragged fetching soft drinks and biscuits. A striking, blond-haired European woman sat in the row in front of him on the other aisle. He tried to eavesdrop for the first hour, without much luck. He overheard her request a glass of champagne. Clearly not a Belgian. Likely Rhodesian or South African. That pinched accent -- polite, informal, direct.

Penderel looked over at her as she sipped the champagne. She had an air of self-importance, tinged with mischievousness. He noticed the red lipstick on the rim of the glass. Her hands were slender, though not prissily manicured. She was a woman who liked being in the center of things.

The woman made conversation with the stewardess, just loud enough to be overheard. Penderel listened, though it was hard to hear exactly what she was saying over the droning hum of the propellers. She turned around sharply and caught his eye. Then looking away, she continued chatting with the stewardess. Penderel felt self-conscious, like a snoop who'd been outed, and he was embarrassed. He was new to the agency, but he was trained better than that.

'First time to Elisabethville?' she turned, walking across the tarmac. 'I tend to know most of the faces. Yours is new. I'm Beryl.' She turned to shake Penderel's hand as they entered the building. The terminal was run-down and warm, with a tattered, water-stained carpet. Several clanking circular fans were placed on the floor. A travel poster with the outline of the continent and a Bedouin man on a camel pointing to the sky welcomed them to Elisabethville. The desert seemed a long way away.

'Yes, it is. Hello, I'm Richard Penderel. Work with the U.S. consulate in Leo.'

Beryl chuckled. 'Ah, the Americans have finally arrived. Hitting the beaches of the great Zambezi. What took you so long? Worried the Belgians are going to screw this up? My husband certainly is.'

Penderel was taken aback at her brashness. She continued walking quickly as they entered the arrivals area. A large man in even larger sunglasses and an olive safari suit stepped forward to take her bag. 'Enjoy your time here, Mr. Penderel. It's a lovely city.' She turned towards him, slowly stepping backwards in her heels, extending her hand.

He grasped it, noting her strong, but feminine hands. 'I'm sure we will see one another again, Mr. Penderel. Believe it or not, this is a small place.' She smiled, turned in stride and disappeared through the front sliding door.

A small man approached him. 'Monsieur Penderel?' Penderel looked up and nodded. 'Welcome to Elisabethville. My name is Etienne. I'm here to take you to Monsieur Biver. Come this way, please.' Etienne took Penderel's small suitcase and they headed out to the car park.

Penderel thought about Beryl. Denman had mentioned in his intial briefing that a number of wealthy white people connected to the mining industry lived here. Penderel assumed that's what her husband did. Mining? Troublemaking? Probably both, he concluded.

'Monsieur,' Etienne interjected, as Penderel sat lost in his thoughts. 'We are at the headquarters.' The drive had been quick and Penderel hadn't even looked out of the window. An imposing rectangular four-story building sat in front of him, as the guard raised the wooden gate and the car proceeded into the parking area next to the front entrance. A large, marble-faced surface chiseled with 'Union Minière du Haut Katanga' sat over the archway.

'Thank you, Etienne,' Penderel answered, still engrossed. *Beryl.*

'Good afternoon.' A tall, well-dressed man in a double-breasted navy suit approached Penderel from across the waiting area. 'Jean-Pierre Biver. It's nice to finally meet you. I trust you had a safe trip?'

'Yes, I did,' Penderel looked up to shake Biver's hand. 'Quite a country to fly across! It's cool here. A nice break from Leo.'

'We're at nearly 4,000 feet. Between here and Leo there's just a lot of jungle … and a few minerals underneath,' he chuckled. 'Lucky for us and for the Belgian Congolese. This is their patrimony, after all. Can I offer you a coffee? Or something stronger?'

'Coffee is fine.'

'What a beautiful place,' Penderel mused as he entered the air-conditioned office, covered with maps, two lion heads, a large antelope of some kind with spiraled horns and an enormous painted calfskin shield. All Penderel could really think of was the obvious power this structure housed.

'Thank you. The work we do here is for the people of Elisabethville,' Biver intoned in a well-rehearsed cadence. 'Our company operates schools, dispensaries, hospitals and sporting clubs. We give back to this community. We even supply electricity and run the railways.' He looked toward Penderel, as he nodded. 'We find the ingredients that make the world run right.'

Penderel expected this. He presumed the next sentence would be, 'And you know, we supply the West with 60 percent of its uranium, 73 percent of its cobalt and 10 percent of its copper.' Instead he paused to light a cigarette as a white-jacketed attendant returned with a large trolley of coffee, tea and small, sticky pastries.

'Please look around this marvelous city while you're here,' he continued. 'We have a brand new university that opened a few years ago. We will have some new graduates in May. Even the Benedictine monks like it here. So much better than poor old Leo. So many grand plans that never will be completed.' He sat back, appearing satisfied.

'Are incomplete construction projects unique to Léopoldville?' Penderel smiled.

Biver shook his head with a chuckle. 'No, sadly, this poor country has little to show for all of the planning. It's an immense place and there is little infrastructure. We've done our best with the railways and bridges, but not enough. Still, you should look around the city.'

'I'm hoping to,' Penderel answered. 'I'm staying over at the Grand for two nights.'

They sat down, facing a low wooden table. 'I understand from your cable that you are new to Belgian Congo. I've met Mr. Timberlake and Mr. Denman several times. I like them both. I think we're all in agreement that we wish to maintain this *very special* relationship between the UMHK and the United States.'

'Yes, Mr. Biver, that is why I am here,' Penderel answered.

'There is a growing *angst* – is that the right term? – that there's going to be upheaval within the next year,' Biver continued. 'Maybe sooner? That crazy nationalist Lumumba is in jail now, but not for long. The conference in Brussels next month will determine how and when independence is decided. My countrymen will push for three to four years. I expect it will be demanded sooner.' Biver stopped and poured himself some coffee from the urn.

'I've heard that perspective, but what specifically are you predicting?' asked Penderel.

Biver smiled quickly. *Surely this chap is not going to make me spell this entire narrative out over afternoon tea?* 'I'm saying that as a strategic customer of ours, the United States needs to plan and be aware of the unexpected consequences that will come from rapid independence. Other parties are already making contingency plans.'

'I would expect so,' said Penderel. 'My role here is to help mitigate the unexpected and to plan for the continuing success of the United States and this country's strategic interests.'

'I think we understand one another then,' Biver nodded. 'Safe to say, there are interests desiring instability. The Union Minière du Haut-Katanga has been an unfailing ally to the United States since before World War I. And as you know, we provided an uninterrupted supply of uranium and cobalt to your country throughout the entire Second World War. Believe me, that was quite a coup of its own that no one speaks about today.'

'Yes, we are very thankful for that. That was *quite* an accomplishment that hasn't gone unnoticed.'

'Oh, by the way, your colleague Mr. Denman and I discussed the purchase of 1,500 tons of uranium oxide as a precautionary measure in case things go awry during this transitional period. We will stockpile it here. One never knows what can happen, but we don't want the Soviets getting their hands on anything.'

'Yes, Mr. Denman and I discussed that issue before I left. We are grateful for your steadfast friendship.'

Penderel stood up, gazed around the large office. He shook Biver's hand and was led down the stairway to the front entrance, where Etienne was waiting.

Penderel sat on the bed at the Grand Hotel. The room was cool, clean and the staff was friendly. He was to join Biver and his wife, Libellule, along with another couple, for dinner at 7:30. The earlier conversation raced through his mind. Sure, there were rumors that the whole Katanga province might secede. Biver had mentioned 'contingency plans' when they spoke. It was tricky to decode tradecraft, though not on this issue.

So far, so good. Penderel's discussion with Biver had gone exactly as Denman had indicated. It was all about loyalty and shared goals. He liked what he saw in Biver – a focused, but gracious man, promoting his company's interests. What Penderel had picked up that was unknowable from the briefs was the quiet and resolute power of the UMHK and the methodical calmness that its leader projected.

He thought back to the five-hour flight and how empty and vast this country is. He remembered night bombing missions over the Korean peninsula that began in Okinawa. There too, there was an emptiness of flying over an ocean at night with only the distant lights of places below that were his targets. Here it was simply a rolling sea of green, punctuated by mist, clouds and far away veins of the great Congo River. There were no markers below. His mind turned to Beryl and her long fingers grasping the champagne flute. What a nice interlude!

Penderel went downstairs to the hotel bar at seven. He was tired from the long flight and wanted to organize his thoughts and send a cable back to Léopoldville. He knew that Denman would be interested in what he was finding out.

The restaurant was empty except for a few white businessmen. He took a seat on a stool and started a conversation with the barman, who seemed startled that a white person would be directly addressing him.

'Good evening, could I get a whiskey and soda, please?'

'Certainly suh. Right away.'

Immediately, the barman returned with the drink, garnished with a lemon and two ice cubes. 'Water has been purified, suh.'

'Please don't call me sir. I'm Richard. Could I get a few more ice cubes?'

'Yes, suh.'

Penderel chuckled, recognizing that establishing informality wasn't going to be easy. Same as back home. His country had its share of racial and class problems. *At least these people are going to get to vote.* Though his job was to be the loyal foot soldier for American interests, his mind occasionally wandered and a lingering sense of hypocrisy bothered him. The United States was in many ways just like Belgian Congo – vast, widely different by region, and controlled by a small, entrenched business elite.

Here he was solving the world's problems when similar ones existed, unaddressed at home. He believed in America's noble mission and its capacity for greatness. After all, he had played a role in stopping the Nazis in Europe and the Red Chinese in Korea less than a decade later.

'There's talk of elections coming up,' Penderel tried to

engage the barman again, looking around the empty bar. It was 7:15. His hosts would be arriving shortly.

'Yes, suh,' the barman answered meekly. 'I'm a supporter of the CONAKAT party. I belong to the Lunda tribe.'

'Do people plan to vote for their tribes?'

'Wah not, suh?' he answered.

'Do you believe in a greater Congo?'

'Wus that?' the barman answered.

Penderel thought to himself, *the guy does have a point.* The concept of a greater, unified Congo was far too abstract to embrace. Its citizens had loyalties to family, tribe and region, not to people who lived 1,000 miles away.

He turned and instantly stirred as two elegantly dressed couples entered the bar. 'Mr. Penderel, lovely to see you,' Biver said. 'I see you're making friends with the locals. This is my wife Libellule.' A very striking, younger, dark-haired woman smiled, nodded and extended her hand. 'And these are the Readers, Beryl and Timothy.'

Penderel tried to mask his exhilaration at seeing Beryl Reader again. 'It's a pleasure to meet you. What a coincidence? I met Mrs. Reader this morning on the plane from Leo.' She looked even better than she did in the morning, all scrubbed and perfumed. A whiff of Vol de Nuit came across the musky, smoke-filled bar. She wore a simple tan linen dress and her blond hair was pulled back.

'Tis a small world,' Biver remarked. 'I thought you'd like to meet some locals. Beryl is a professor of geology at our university. We're so lucky to have her. Timothy works in the Northern Rhodesian consulate. And my Libellule keeps all of us honest.'

'That, I suspect, is a big job!' Penderel teased. A hushed, awkward silence followed, until Biver interjected, 'Who's hungry?'

'So how are you finding the Belgian Congo so far?' Beryl asked, lighting a cigarette as the waiter cleared the plates from the table. 'Have you been able to get out and see the country? It's quite spectacular.'

'No, it's been all work so far. Just trying to meet a few people. Hopefully tomorrow I can look around this city.'

'What is it you do?' she asked.

'Diplomacy. We've always relied on the Belgians in this part of the world. But the winds are shifting.'

'Indeed,' said Timothy Reader. He had a thick Rhodesian accent and a burly build. He clearly spent time outdoors and used his hands. 'Jean-Pierre has heard this a lot so he won't be offended. The Belgians have been asleep at the switch.'

Biver quietly nodded. 'It's always easy to view the world in hindsight. The pieces all fit. What we're trying to do here is prepare this promising country for the future.'

Penderel looked over at Biver and Reader. There was a placid confidence in their expressions, as though the future had already happened. 'Tell me about your work at the university,' Penderel said, turning to Beryl. His face was flushed from the wine and an uncomfortable awareness of her.

'Whatever the Congolese ultimately decide,' she replied, 'they'll need to understand what's underneath them. These rocks in the ground are their future. What is briarite? Coretite? Cobalt? And what is their use? Do you know the answer, Mr. Penderel?' she asked coyly.

'I'm afraid I'm not much of a geology student. But I am a quick learner.'

Beryl smiled, then continued. 'I teach intro geology and another course on extraction technologies. How do we get this bloody stuff out of the ground? Pretty useful skills for an emerging country, wouldn't you say?

'Mr. Penderel, despite your lack of education, I suspect you know what cobalt and briarite are used for?'

'Yes, I have a faint notion,' he smiled looking over at Biver. 'I believe those are the ingredients that make the world run right?'

'Quite good, Mr. Penderel,' Beryl answered, smoke curling around her blond coiffed head. 'You *are* a quick learner.'

'I'm just a good listener. Mr. Biver was good enough to give me lesson one this afternoon.' Biver looked over and laughed with politely cheerful applause.

'And Timothy, how about you?' Penderel continued contentedly. 'What is your line of work?'

'I work for the protectorate in commercial relations,' Reader answered without elaboration.

Libellule turned to Penderel, staring intensely. 'What do you expect will happen over the next year? Surely, the Americans have a perspective.' Her dark hair was pulled back off her long, elegant neck. There was something standoffish and superior about her that bugged Penderel.

'We really do not know,' Penderel began, trying to choose his words precisely. He was tired and slightly drunk. 'My personal guess is that the upcoming roundtable talks will be a disaster. Kasavubu and the Abakos will demand too much too soon. Belgium will refuse -- then capitulate -- knowing it has no leverage. I expect full independence and elections by the end of 1960.'

Biver and Reader laughed, raising a glass. Biver toasted, 'Here, here to our new friend. I think your analysis is pretty accurate. But the political parties are fractious. I bet they will demand elections within six months.'

'Perhaps,' said Penderel. 'It will make all of our lives very difficult.' He looked over at Reader, who had a smirk on his face.

'When are you headed back?' Biver asked.

'Early Wednesday,' Penderel answered. 'As you know, the flight schedule isn't all that frequent.'

'There's someone I'd like you to meet tomorrow,' Biver said. 'Very sharp guy. He's one of the few people in this country who can read a balance sheet. His name is Moise Tshombe. You've heard of him?' he asked teasingly.

Penderel smiled. 'Probably a few thousand times, yes. An introduction? That would be terrific.'

Moise Tshombe entered the UMHK office building at 9:30 and took the elevator to the third floor. He knew where he was going. He had the physical presence of a leader, with a large animated face, high bushy eyebrows and a big smile. He spoke with perfect diction and dressed elegantly in a grey chalk-striped suit with a silk pocket square to match his tie. He extended his hand and gripped Penderel's firmly.

'It is a pleasure to meet you, Mr. Penderel. Mr. Timberlake mentioned that you were arriving in country. Welcome to Katanga.

'This is fortuitous,' Tshombe continued. 'I am heading to Europe right after Christmas for holiday, then on to Brussels for the conference.'

Biver stepped in and invited them to sit down. 'I thought this would be a good opportunity for you to get acquainted. Lots of big events coming up.'

'Indeed,' said Penderel. 'Mr. Tshombe, I'd love to hear your views on the upcoming conference.' Denman had cautioned him not to be too solicitous, but the occasion seemed right.

Tshombe smiled. 'Please call me Moise. It's a Hebrew name – a variant of Moses.' His baritone voiced filled the large office space.

'Have you too been put here to lead your people out of slavery?' Penderel asked kiddingly. He felt comfortable with this large, self-confident man, though he wished he hadn't used the slavery term.

Tshombe let out a belly laugh. 'That's quite good. Yes, I guess I am. I'll need to use that in my upcoming campaign.' He chuckled again and shifted in his chair. His face was dark in the large office, but his eyes were large and bright.

'Mr. Penderel, I am very concerned about this conference,' Tshombe began. 'My countrymen are not prepared for independence. We're too tribal, and there are not enough educated people to hold so large a country together.'

'So that is why you support a federalized Congo?' said Penderel.

'Yes, it is all we can handle. And frankly, I have my doubts about that. There is one more thing that concerns me. The Soviet Union. They have been making efforts to connect with us, particularly with Gizenga and Lumumba. They see an opening.

'I hope the U.S. does as well,' he continued. 'Our relationship dates back to the twenties. I've had encouraging conversations with Mr. Denman and Mr. Timberlake on helping us with the transition.' He slowly moved his enormous left hand to his chin, showing a starched french cuff, an onyx link and a Patek Philippe watch.

'Yes, Mr. Tshombe,' Penderel answered. 'We too are concerned with Soviet efforts to infiltrate Africa. I spoke to Mr. Biver about this and I assured him that the United States will do everything it can to retain Congo in the Christian, western orbit.'

Tshombe looked pleased and smiled at Penderel. 'That is very reassuring. We will call on the United States to help us through our infancy and we, in turn, will remain loyal allies and strategic partners.'

A professional, well-oiled machine, Penderel thought, looking out of the window of the DC-7 on his return flight to Léopoldville the next morning -- Tshombe, Biver, the UMHK, the social circle, the supporting infrastructure – all of it. Katanga really was where the action was going to be in this country. Their power and systems for maintaining it were the practical counterpoints to anything that could happen in Léopoldville. He found their confidence and disregard for the inevitable changes in the future arrogant, but oddly reassuring. In a country where everyone else was nervous, Penderel had met the smart, wealthy and prepared.

Five

Late December 1959

Penderel sat in the bar at the Memling Hotel, drinking his third whisky and soda. It was Christmas Eve. Most of the consulate staff with families had left for holiday and Léopoldville was a steamy ghost town. Denman had gone to London to meet his wife and teenage daughter. Timberlake was in the States for ten days. Only he and Leon Tucci, Deputy Chief of Station, remained on post – the bachelors taking the graveyard shift. Tucci was due to join him any minute now. It was almost eight. Christmas carols were playing over the radio and the consulate was going to be closed tomorrow. It was a perfect night to get drunk.

He saw Tucci enter the bar. He was not yet thirty, energetic, clean-shaven and well-dressed. Penderel had grown to like him. His sharp sense of humor, cockiness and perceptiveness were appealing traits – a perfect post-war American envoy. He had a second-generation

American's hunger for devouring all that was thrown at him and was the kind of person who never looked back, never had regrets.

Tucci's grandparents had emigrated from Sicily to New York at the turn of the century not speaking a word of English. Both his parents went to college and his father started a very successful heating and air conditioning business outside Pittsburgh. Leon and his sister went to Ivy League schools. Though he never lost the tough-guy swagger, he was smooth, cosmopolitan and addicted to opera.

Tucci's rise in the agency had been swift. He had joined the Foreign Service in 1952, straight out of Princeton. His brown, steady eyes twinkled when he told jokes, but there was an underlying seriousness and honesty. This young guy worked very hard and was clearly going places.

'Good evening,' Tucci said, walking in. 'And Merry Christmas.'

'Same to you,' Penderel replied. 'Can I get you a drink? I'm wary of the egg nog.'

'Thanks. I'll have what you're having.' Tucci looked over and motioned to the bartender, sitting absentmindedly on a stool, picking his teeth with a swizzle stick. They were the only patrons in the bar. 'Make it a double,' Tucci said, eying Penderel's empty glass.

'Where's home?' Penderel asked.

'Shadyside, near Pittsburgh. Sorry not to be there. They had a snowstorm over the weekend. I love that first snow of the winter. Never thought I'd say 'I love the snow.' And you?'

'Originally from Richmond, Virginia. Not much snow there. But I was in the air force, so I've spent many Christmas Eves like this. Though not one this tropical.'

'Sounds sad. Boy, is that a plea to Santa Claus?' Tucci answered, throwing his scotch back and requesting another. 'I've missed a few myself. We're out here on the lonely edge of civilization, looking out for the homeland. It's a noble pursuit.'

'What do you make of this place so far?'

'Hard to tell. It's a tough place to get your arms around. So much is muddled and unsettled. The upcoming conference, the politicians, the Belgians – it's all bouncing around without any rhythm of how it will come together.

'Everyone here thinks of themselves as royalty,' Tucci continued. 'Lumumba's a gasbag who fancies himself a king. Tshombe *is* a king. This is like medieval Europe. You've met Tshombe? I hear he is quite impressive.'

'Yes, I met him earlier this month. I liked him, a jolly confident man, but he's counting on us for protection. Very tricky thing to pull off,' Penderel answered, stubbing out his cigarette. 'We're for freedom and democracy, just so long as it benefits us.'

Tucci looked up, head askance. His eyes narrowed as he took a deep drag off his cigarette. 'Sadly, our job is not to be politicians or to have an opinion. We're just taking orders and carrying out policy someone else is deciding. Some of that is very liberating. Some of it, though, will swing around and bite us in the ass.'

'I know, boy, do I know,' Penderel laughed. 'I've been a soldier my whole life. I've never disobeyed an order, though I have questioned many of them. We bombed villages all over Germany, never a military vehicle in sight. You still have family back in Pittsburgh?'

'Yeah, my parents live there. I have two sisters, too. One's married. The other's single and lives in New York. My folks' place is near a golf course that has a big hill. Practically lived on that hill as a kid all winter long. Was just thinking about sledding down it. Christmas should be about sleighrides, not drinking in some sad bar. How 'bout you?'

'Both of my parents are dead,' Penderel said. 'Never got married. Was in the airforce for fifteen years and never got around to falling in love. Kinda got used to being alone.'

'Sorry to hear that. Well, I'm your family tonight. Cheers and merry Christmas!'

They motioned to the bartender for another round. 'I

admire your ability to speak French so fluently,' said Penderel. His words came out like *speck flinch so fruently.*

'I might need to get a double to catch up,' Tucci smiled, motioning to the bartender to pour another jigger into the short glass, before he returned. 'I took it in college and then it got better in Tehran. Can't read Persian for shit.'

'What's Iran like now the Shah's back?' asked Penderel. He downed his drink and rested his shoulders against the back of the padded barstool. 'Seems like they're some parallels between Mosaddeq and Lumumba. You know, two nationalists fighting colonial powers? Both fueled by resentment. Both sitting on a shitpile of natural resources.' He was impressed how the steady flow of Dewars White Label had brought clarity to his thinking.

'Yeah, there are parallels,' answered Tucci, lighting a cigarette, motioning to the bartender for another round. It was nearing 11 p.m. and theirs were the only voices to be heard on the first floor of the Hotel Memling. 'Big difference is, there's been a Persian culture for thousands of years. Art, culture, science and literature. But Mosaddeq was going to drive it into the ground and we had to do something.'

'No monarch-in-waiting to unite and lead this place forward,' said Penderel with a slight hiccup. He signaled the barman for the check.

'Remember everyone is a king here,' smiled Tucci,

throwing back the last of the scotch. 'Which makes no one a king.'

The bill paid, Tucci and Penderel stumbled out into the steamy night. The city was eerily quiet, except for the soft melody of 'Good King Wencelaus' drifting out of a second-story window. There were cheap paper decorations affixed to a few doors. The two men shook hands and parted ways for the evening.

Six

January 1960

Penderel couldn't sleep. The conference in Brussels had been going on for over a week without any resolution. He and his colleagues at the consulate felt powerless to do anything. The fucking stupid Belgians! They were insisting on a three-to-four year transition period. Everyone in the Congolese delegation, except Tshombe, wanted it right away. He, Timberlake and Denman had tried to convince Rene Delvaux that this would happen. And also that Lumumba would try to steal the limelight. Dumb ass egomaniac!

He went to the window in his small flat off Boulevarde de Pais. It was quiet outside, except for a cheerless barking dog and the tortured screech of a gearbox of a car with a broken clutch. The driver was likely drunk or high on hootch. There were a few boys out on the street up to no good, but thankfully, they looked to be moving toward another neighborhood.

The decisions being reached 4,000 miles away would be so consequential to life outside his window, but there was no evidence of that now. In a few months, these same boys might be carrying Kalishnikovs. Or serving in the military? Or dead in the street?

Penderel gazed at the scene and imagined a different Léopoldville – a lawless street, different tribes fighting against one another, no one really in charge, Belgians fleeing the country by the planeload. They were done here, except maybe in Katanga. And they will fight to the end to keep Katanga, he was certain of that.

Before him, he saw a de facto federation where the capital exerted little control. He saw the Soviets fomenting trouble, supporting mini-revolutions, trying to get their hands on the uranium and cobalt – the ultimate prize that mattered more than lives lost. He remembered the protesters with the Russian AK-47's the morning he arrived two months earlier.

Penderel got dressed without showering. Hot water was intermittent, anyway. The two-block walk to the consulate took three minutes. He noticed most of the lights were on in the building. Denman, Tucci and Jerry, the new ham radio guy they just hired, were all there, anxious and unable to sleep.

'Good evening, gentlemen,' Penderel said, walking through the front door by the dozing guard on duty. 'Or rather, I should say, good morning. I couldn't sleep. What's your excuse?'

'The same,' Denman muttered. The small office was cluttered with files and crumpled-up telexes. The smell of cigarettes and too many sweaty men inside a confined space was nauseating. Tucci looked up from the telex machine. 'They want to know if we know anything.'

'Hell, they're closer to the action than we are!' Denman answered, exhaling nearly half of the Chesterfield he'd just taken in. 'They've got a roomful of analysts in Langley and they're asking us? Geez!'

Tucci jumped in. 'The Congolese are just waiting them out. Time is on their side. The Belgians will eventually say 'fine' and be done with it. Picking up anything, Jerry?'

'No sir,' he answered. 'A lot of noise out there, though.'

'I made a fresh pot of coffee. Anyone want some?' Tucci asked.

'Sure.'

A coded cable came in a little before 8:00 in the morning from the State Department. Denman stood up and began reading it on the machine. 'Oh shit. They finally made a deal, a big bad one. The Belgians agreed to hold elections by May 22nd with independence granted on June 30th.'

Penderel slumped in his chair. *Four months to get this place ready for independence. Oh my God!*

Seven

Early February 1960

Penderel became friendly with a Lebanese restaurant owner, Habib Khouri. He had a small, but elegant place, Le Restaurant Cedars Élevé, near the consulate that was favored by many of the Europeans. Penderel liked his energetic, solicitous manner and delicious French-inspired cuisine. Khouri had moved to Léopoldville in his late-thirties after the war and the partitioning of Palestine and creation of Israel. As a Christian, he bore no enemies here. He had developed a loyal expat clientele who missed their béchamel sauces and crème brûlées. He also became Penderel's operative.

They met in November when Penderel first arrived, after he had put in another twelve-hour-day. The restaurant was empty and all he wanted was a stiff drink, some soft cheese, a few olives and a baguette to gnaw on. They started talking.

'This country is my home,' Habib began, as he cleared the plates and refilled Penderel's short glass with Dewar's.

'The Belgians took me in with open arms and my children were born here. In many ways, it's a lot more civilized than what happened in the Middle East after the war, though it's the same story. Too many tribes trying to grab land and resources. Look at Lebanon! It's already fracturing. But I do worry what will happen when the white people leave here.'

'Well, you may be a position to help us with the transition.' Penderel said. He sensed Habib had a willingness to help.

'Perhaps,' Habib answered slowly, though not warily. 'I love the Belgians, but they do not know how to guide a country. They are split in two parts, right? The Flemish and the Walloons. They can barely hold together a place the size of your state of Maryland,' he laughed.

Penderel was excited to recruit his very first operative. He had been trained on how to do it – the slow, meticulous exchanges; the small talk that became the foundation for trust and larger talk. Larger talk that finally leads to an agreement.

But still, training exercises were just that. He knew that there was no substitute for the real experience and the chance for rejection. When a potential operative was formally approached, the answer had to be 'yes' before the question was asked. And this was important for Richard Penderel personally.

For all of his accomplishments on the battlefield, he

was a middle-aged man in an entry-level job he had limited preparation for. He was envious of the world-weary Denman and Tucci – their experiences, their education, their training, and their understanding of how the clandestine world really worked. Penderel felt like a fraud some days, pushed to the front of the class by reason of his heroism and technical skill at shooting a gun from the rear of a cold plane. That didn't take intelligence. In fact, that took the opposite.

'I will help you, Mr. Penderel,' Habib quietly stated one evening. 'The only thing I ask is when the fighting starts – and it will start, I'm sure of that – that the United States will evacuate my family to Brazzaville. I will stay. Agreed?'

Penderel nodded.

'Well, the first thing I will tell you that I overheard last week is that the Soviets are increasing their influence here, starting with Lumumba. Two Greeks occasionally come in and I often eavesdrop.'

'That's very useful information, Habib,' he answered. 'How many languages do you speak?'

'Six. English, Arabic, French, a little German, some Bantu and Greek,' he answered proudly. 'One has to be fluent with a lot of things to live in Lebanon.'

'I'll call you next week. We'll establish some protocols for regularly connecting. Thank you, Habib.'

All of the consulate staff quickly tried to dig into the dirt of the political landscape. With elections in four months, it was going to be a sprint, with a lot of guesswork. That no one in this country had ever tried to form a political coalition was the first of many problems. At least in the French and British African colonies, there were efforts to form two-party systems. Not here.

The result was a proliferation of small parties, mostly based on region or tribe, with little encouragement toward compromise or the sharing of power. There were signs that the Belgian Congo would become a tropical shit storm.

Being American was like having a sandwich board stuck over your shoulders. The locals could see you coming and knew what you were selling. Still, several individuals were willing to exchange information, either for their own skins or the betterment of the new country – provided, of course, there were incentives.

As Station Chief, George Denman's responsibility was to get to know Patrice Lumumba, the head of the one quasi-national party, the *Mouvement National Congolais*, and his omnipresent deputy, Joseph Mobutu. The MNC-L party was the frontrunner for control of the legislature and he was expected to be the country's first prime minister.

But Lumumba was unpredictable and Denman's style wasn't necessarily well matched for making deals with a dramatic populist, who peppered most conversations with 'resentment of the West.' When they initially met,

Lumumba's first words were, 'So the U.S. is now in charge of our enslavement?'

Denman was warned about this rhetoric and urged not to overreact. They were likely going to have to work with him. But Lumumba rarely remembered exactly what he said. He'd just utter another inflammatory insult.

Always agile, Lumumba had a politician's innate flair for self-promotion, bouncing along the surface, changing course to suit the moment. He was thin and photogenic, and used his large, bony hands forcefully and elegantly, like the conductor of an orchestra. His big problem was he couldn't read the music, nor did he always know what key to be in.

Denman had met Patrice Lumumba a few times, but Lumumba was not interested in other viewpoints. He was enraptured with his own voice and his crusading antipathy towards Belgium and the European colonial powers infused every conversation. His expressions and dramatic gestures signaled passion, but fragility and impatience, too. His national party would likely win the most seats, but governing would be far different than winning an election.

There was another piece of the puzzle that Denman needed to figure out how to fit in – Joseph-Désiré Mobutu. Formerly an army conscript and journalist, Mobutu served as a personal aide and advisor to Patrice Lumumba. Everyone agreed that this was an extremely intelligent man, very young, perhaps immature, but a person with great potential. He had practically taken over the Belgian conference three weeks earlier amid Lumumba's theatrical prancing.

Penderel's was assigned two young rising politicians to get to know and hopefully form close relationships with. They were Justin Bomboko, a politician from the northwest and Victor Nendaka, who had formed his own MNC-Nendaka party, after a falling out with the flighty Lumumba. He also had responsibility for Tshombe, Biver and Katanga, to the extent anyone had any influence over what they did.

Penderel first met Bomboko at the Metropole bar at the Le Regina Hotel. Bomboko was dancing arm-in-arm with a woman on an outdoor patio, broadly grinning to cheers from onlookers. He was a short, stocky man, with a round, animated face and absorbing, intelligent eyes. He had the reputation of being a ladies' man and was a regular fixture at the bar. But he was thoughtful, well-read and extremely quick in assessing people and situations. Penderel liked him instantly. They sat down and Penderel bought him a beer.

A week later, Penderel met him again at the bar and they struck up a conversation. 'I come from the Équateur Province and I am a chief to the Mongo people,' Bomboko began. 'We are all aligned with our tribes, which is something the Belgians have understood all too well. No one can rule a country as disconnected as the Congo. We're the second largest ethnic group in the country, but we have no voice.'

'Democracy is messy,' Penderel countered. 'But it is essential for Congo to become independent and free from colonial rule. Look at the United States!'

'Ah, Mr. Penderel,' he smiled, taking a large swig from the glass. 'Your country fought wars against the British, your native Indians, the French, the Spaniards, the Mexicans, and finally yourselves in your first eighty years of independence. Is that what we can look forward to?' He laughed as his broad face expanded, but his eyes never left Penderel's.

'You make a good point, sir,' Penderel mused. 'A very good point.'

'This will be a rough election and an even rougher post-independence period,' Bomboko continued. 'Already you can see we have three MNL parties running. *Three?* No one can read! What kind of a country has a MNC-L, a MNC-K and a MNC-N on the ballot? It's stupid!'

'You had your Federalists, led by Alexander Hamilton, who promoted city and business interests,' he continued. 'And you had Thomas Jefferson and his Republican party. They were concerned about state's rights. Your decisions were clear. Two choices with different philosophies.'

'You're quite a scholar of U.S. history,' Penderel remarked. 'I'm afraid your grasp is far better than mine. I never finished high school.'

'One thing you will need to do is to see this country,' urged Bomboko. 'People say it is this great expanse the size of Europe. Maybe so, but it is the last piece of the continent that anyone wanted. The geography is harsh and the rivers are unnavigable. Sadly, the Congo River is better for books than for trading. The 'Heart of Darkness' is a very fitting description for our land.'

Penderel was introduced to Victor Nendaka in late January after the Brussels conference through Denman who met him the prior summer. He was quiet and studious, preferring books and the company of his family to drinking and dancing.

Nendaka was self-taught and had a sharp, inquisitive mind. He was outspoken that the United States was essential to his new country's future success and had no affection for Belgium.

'It's time for them to go home, make beer and chocolate and take their little peeing boy statue with them,' he'd said in their first meeting.

In addition to getting to know Justin Bomboko and Victor Nendaka, Penderel liked his other responsibility -- visiting the clean, orderly Katanga province, where

Tshombe was all but certain to win control of the legislature. Biver and Tshombe always made time for him. Plus there was Beryl Reader.

His infatuation for Beryl made Penderel instantly wary of her fifteen-stone husband, Timothy. He had the thick, thuggish look of ex-military, though he had the polish of a man used to the finer things in life. He had a splotchy, freckled face, coarse blond eyebrows and sun-bleached hair. His hands were tough and callused.

For his part, Jean-Pierre Biver was completely transparent about his priorities. He was the puppetmaster after all, doling out money that would be reinvested in his corporation, one way or another. The secretive nature of the UMHK intrigued many, but no one dared to try to put the maze of politics, money and power together. Biver knew that uttering the word 'uranium' to the right audience could keep the world at bay.

Still, there was something admirable about Jean-Pierre Biver. He was courtly, yet solicitious. He was charged with running a company at the behest of investors for its owner, the Société Générale de Belgique. He spent his early career building railway bridges across southern Africa and Brazil. Penderel liked his precision and thoroughness. In this uncertain, shifting world, Biver seemed to be the one consistently predictable individual he could count on, for better or worse.

So when Penderel and Denman received an invitation

from Biver to join him, his wife Libellule, the Readers and a few other select friends for a weekend of hunting at a farm along the Rhodesian border, Penderel quickly agreed.

Eight

Late February 1960

Denman was very quiet on their commercial flight to Elisabethville. That bugged Penderel. *This guy was moody.* One minute, he could be passionate and opinionated; other times, he was introverted and secretive. Penderel had learned to give him wide berth in the four months he'd reported to him. Just as he had a bad sense about Reader and a good, almost trusting feeling toward Rene Delvaux, Penderel felt something about his boss that made him uncomfortable.

Penderel's insecurity about his qualifications had faded with experience and success in establishing fruitful relationships. But he remained cautious and wary that Denman saw him as an overrated fraud, who'd been foisted upon him without the depth of knowledge or training to be a field agent.

Penderel believed that this would be an interesting

weekend. The word *interesting* covered all sorts of ground. To see these characters on their home turf with their guards relaxed could be helpful in better understanding the larger picture.

Would he get some alone time to flirt with Beryl? He hoped so. He'd surely get a closer assessment of her husband and what made their relationship tick. In the few meetings they'd had, there was nothing obvious.

Penderel wondered about the other guests. He guessed there would be a collection of white military types, men who knew how to shoot a gun and drink into the night. Maybe some Belgian viscounts and other colonial neer-do-wells who hadn't felt the winds of change blowing across the continent?

He peered out of the window as the plane banked to the right to align for its initial approach into Elisabethville. Coming out of the repetitive vista of thick green mist, the sight of the drier, harsher highlands was a relief. He thought back to his lengthy approach into Leo back in November. Then he had watched the large, languid, lazy light brown snake, the Congo River, curling through the empty emerald landscape. It was the central artery that all other rivers and streams drained into, enormous, violent and unpredictable, capable of expelling humankind. It had ceded little ground as of March 1961 to anyone in history.

Penderel realized that he had seen the world from above, its quiet beauty and magnificence devoid of human beings. It was just shapes and colors and contrasts. It was like that at night over northern Europe and the Korean peninsula. Just the tiny lights of civilization plotted out across the landscape, so inconsequential and innocent. The lives below were so far away, which helped his conscience on bombing missions. The Belgian Congo too was distant, but powerful, physically dominant. The jungle would always hold the upper hand.

Denman sat across the aisle, underlining pertinent portions of briefs that he had brought with him. His satchel was small and orderly. He had William Shirer's *The Rise and Fall of the Third Reich* and Gunter Grass's *The Tin Drum* neatly stacked in his open briefcase on the empty seat.

Penderel smiled. Two different takes on World War II. Intense guy. Denman looked up and smiled quickly, sensing he was being observed. 'Looks like we're landing soon.' He checked his watch and then went back to his underlining.

Penderel had been reading *The Flame Trees of Thika.* Huxley's descriptions of the East African landscape gave poetry to the vista below him. He noted one and underlined it with the blue BIC pen he was carrying in his breast pocket.

'This was a moment of magic revealing to us all, for a few moments, a hidden world of grace and wonder beyond the one of which our eyes told us, a world that no words could delineate, as insubstantial as a cloud, as iridescent as a dragon-fly and as innocent

as the heart of a rose.'

'A hidden world of grace and wonder …' that was it. *That was it,*' he joyfully thought to himself.

As the pilot gunned the engines for the landing, he noticed two Land Rovers and a truck alongside the tarmac. There was military precision in how they were lined up – neatly spaced, equipped by neatly dressed black men in khaki shorts and knee socks. Three women in large straw hats waved as the plane landed. The hunting party would soon begin. He felt a sharp pain in his stomach. *Butterflies for Beryl*, he smiled.

Penderel and Denman descended the metal stairway to the tarmac and immediately one of the Land Rovers drove over. A tall, dark man greeted them, 'Welcome to Elisabethville, Mr. Denman and Mr. Penderel. We're delighted to have you. It's good to see you again, Mr. Denman.'

Denman looked up with a quick smile and nodded. The spit-polished greeter carefully put their bags into a small towed trailer and drove to the edge of the runway.

'Good afternoon, gentlemen. Welcome back to Katanga,' Beryl greeted them with an outstretched hand. 'You've both met Libellule before. And this is Doris. Her husband Harold is Belgian minister for African Affairs.'

'It's a pleasure to meet you both.' Doris said, lowering

her stylish tortoise-shell sunglasses, extending her hand. She looked to be an athletic forty with pale skin and high cheekbones. Her auburn-colored hair was pulled back stylishly, resting on the pressed collar of a blindingly white buttoned-down shirt. She was wearing pale khaki jodhpurs and a brown, tooled leather belt with an enormous silver buckle, more befitting a Texas oil baroness than a cultured European colonial.

'We're the advance party,' said Beryl, as the corps of support staff stood formally. 'We will get you settled in at Elysium. It's only about an hour drive south. Our husbands will be arriving later. They would be here, but you as know, business calls.

'Mr. Denman and Mr. Penderel, please ride with Armand and me in this Rover. Doris and Libellule should ride with Francis. You'll have more room. Shadrack will follow with the luggage and supplies. It's a beautiful afternoon. Let's keep the top down. It's not too dusty.

'We are headed for my special place, my heaven and Eden all wrapped in one,' Beryl began as they pulled onto the two-lane highway, heading south. 'It belonged to my parents. My father came here in 1910. He too was involved in mining. They call the area we are going to 'The Copperbelt.' Like Katanga, we have always put the natives first. We give them jobs, housing, healthcare and education. Much more than most white Africans. Would either of you care for any champagne?'

Denman looked up briefly, shaking his head. 'I'd love to join you,' Penderel said. *To hell with this stiff.*

'Armand, could you pull over up ahead and retrieve that bottle of Tattinger from the ice box and two glasses?' Beryl looked relaxed and radiant, as the waning sun crossed her large hat and illuminated her tanned skin and white teeth.

'Yes, ma'am.'

'Are you sure, Mr. Denman? It's Friday afternoon. The workweek is over now. Or is it ever over for gentlemen in your profession?' Her eyes had locked onto Penderel's and part of her mouth turned up in playful conspiratorial confidence.

'Oh well, yes, then,' Denman answered, distracted and defeated. 'I suspect it is time to enjoy the weekend.'

'Three glasses, Armand,' Beryl called. 'How delightful! And from this point on, we're to go by given names. I'm Beryl, you are George and Richard. No need to continue with this dance of formality.'

'Yes, Beryl,' Denman answered, suitably scolded.

'If that's the case,' Penderel jumped in. 'Please call me Dicky.'

The two-lane road heading south was empty, except for a few belching trucks prodding along in the opposite direction. The land was sere and every fifteen minutes they passed a settlement of mud and thatch huts. Cows stared out at the roadway. Young, tall men nodded as the three vehicles passed by. They crossed into Northern Rhodesia, past a forlorn gatehouse, waved past by a bored border guard.

They arrived at Elysium a little before 5 p.m. The modest white gates to the farm sat amongst a thicket of trees that wound down along a creek. 'Do you know what Elysium is?' Beryl asked Denman.

'I believe it is the place in Greek mythology where good people go after they die. A sort of heaven.'

'Very good, George,' Beryl answered. 'You *are* well educated. Wasn't your father a university professor?'

'He was,' Denman replied, looking surprised. 'You certainly screen your guests well.'

Beryl grinned. 'Thank you, George. One must have a thirst for knowledge to keep up out here on the edge of civilization. Your respective backgrounds are impressive. But then what is public isn't always indicative of what lies beneath the surface. I've found that true in both people and geology.' She had lowered her sunglasses to the tip of her nose, revealing her sharp, spritely eyes.

Penderel was already tight from the champagne. Denman had finished one glass, yet the bottle was empty. Beryl's face was flushed, but she didn't appear to have lost her gift to make conversations flow and men attracted to her.

Penderel happily looked out of the car window to the fierce contrasting ochres, greens and purples radiant in the dusky light. The hills in the distance provided a jagged line that separated the darkening foreground from the fuchsia and plum sky. The breeze was cool and his mind was free.

Beryl interrupted the silence. 'The farm extends out over eighty square kilometers,' she said pointing off to the left. 'We employ 85 people, but probably take care of close to 300. We look after lots of extended families. We grow maize and cotton mostly. The rear portion is leased to the Anglo-American Corporation. There's one small copper mine that helps defray the upkeep. But all and all, this is a virtuous circle. We provide a life to the people of northwest Northern Rhodesia.'

'How about Timothy?' asked Penderel.

'Oh, Timothy's family is also from this area. His grandfather was among the first to arrive here in the 1880s. A dear friend of Cecil Rhodes. Timothy fought for the Crown up in Tanganyika against the Germans. We met at university right after the war.'

The Land Rover crossed over a small bridge and ahead on a sloping hill sat 'Elysium.' The sign sat at the turnoff, a white shield, with dark green scripted letters painted on the face. A low-slung Dutch-colonial mud-brick structure with a glistening wall of white-mullioned windows and doors and a red-tiled roof sat contentedly in the cool sun up on the hill. An army of workers tending to the planted fields waved as the truck kicked up dust along the serpentine driveway. 'Ah, I believe I would never tire of coming up this driveway,' Beryl sighed. 'This is where my spirit will live after I die.'

'I can understand why,' said Denman, taking in the vista. Five tall men stood at attention in khaki uniforms as the three vehicles pulled up.

'Mwasewela bwanji. Kunena moni abwenzi kwa Amereka,' Beryl beamed.

'Moni,' the group shouted in unison.

'They are saying 'hello.'

The porters quickly gathered the luggage from the boots of the Land Rovers. 'Please take our guests' bags to their bedrooms.'

Beryl led her four guests out onto the veranda that faced the foothills. The bright orange sun had expanded as it began to drop behind the cobalt blue rise in the distance. One of the servants had opened another bottle of champagne and was pouring flutes.

'Out there,' she said pointing toward the horizon, 'is where you will hunt tomorrow. There may be the odd lion or buffalo, but mostly we see antelope. Sables are the most valued. See?' Beryl pointed to the enormous chestnut head with white markings on the outside wall. A pair of four-foot horns arched back from the head.

'I'm not much of a hunter myself,' she continued, 'though I did kill a small gazelle when I was a child. There were a big herd of them and I just fired a .410 into the crowd. Not very sporting, I must admit.

'Are you a hunter, Richard?' she continued. Denman and the two ladies looked up. Two of them had heard this repartee before. 'I know you did some aerial shooting back in the war.'

'No, not really, but I like a good sporting afternoon on the ground. More of a bird hunter, I guess.'

Overhead, the silence of the rolling plain was broken with a shriek of a loud aircraft above the treetops. 'Oh, here come the boys!' Beryl said, pointing to the sky.

Penderel and Denman looked up agape, pointing. 'Good to know they need a fighter wing to bring them in,' said Penderel quietly to Penderel over the racket. A French-built Fouga Magister buzzed the farm, along with an armed Alouette II helicopter. Thirty seconds later, a single-engine plane came over across the sky. 'Gee whiz,' Penderel pointed at the roar coming towards him. 'That's a T-6 Texan! She's a long way from home.' He looked puzzled as the plane whooshed 200 feet over him at 200 miles per hour.

Denman looked up, finishing up one of his seemingly

always-lit cigarettes. 'They certainly know how to travel in these parts. But where do they land?'

'There's a good-sized bush airstrip a few miles away. They'll be here in fifteen minutes,' Beryl replied. 'Several of the mining companies use it.'

This really is another world. Three military aircraft to bring in three businessmen. The secret world of the powerful and blessed, Penderel thought.

Penderel strolled around the grounds, waiting for dinner. He had showered and put on his white dinner jacket, glad to finally to have the opportunity to wear it. It was nearing 8 p.m. and the afternoon sky had turned pitch-black. He looked back to the farmhouse, brightly lit and bustling, glasses clanking and the faint sound of 'La vie en rose' rising over the deafening chorus of crickets in the trees.

'Dicky, I wondered where you were,' proclaimed Denman as he walked onto the lawn, just outside the glow of the house lights. 'Don't go too far. We'd hate to lose you to a leopard.'

Penderel looked up, suddenly. Denman had made a joke and he looked like a different person. 'This is quite a place. Have you been here before?'

'Once last year. With Tshombe,' Denman answered,

drawing his cigarette down. 'It's their little clubhouse.'

'What's with all of the aircraft?' Penderel asked. For the first time, Denman looked like a spy. Or at least, a version of Humphrey Bogart *playing a spy* -- a small, fit man in a white dinner jacket, dark hair slicked back, tugging on a cigarette. Before he had never thought of Denman as fitting the profile. An overworked, underappreciated accountant, maybe?

'Well, it's a question I haven't dared to ask,' he said. 'Probably's bad form. But now you see what this world is all about. Our job is to stay close, listen hard, stay grateful and never suggest there is one inch between our mutual goals.'

'I think our hostess may enjoy her bubbly?' Penderel said, looking back at the house and terrace. He could hear Beryl's dominating voice above Edith Piaf.

'Yes, I was noticing the same thing. She has a thing for you. Be careful.'

'Me? Nah. She's a flirt and I'm a new face,' Penderel said, watching Denman shake his head.

'Her husband is not a man worth crossing. The Belgians are scared of him. He plays only to Tshombe. Be careful. Don't drink too much and you might learn something.'

'I won't and I will, boss.'

'OK, I get to sit between our newest guests, Mr. Denman and Mr. Penderel,' Beryl announced. 'Hostess makes the rules. I mean I get to sit next to Richard and George, our new friends.'

'I can't ever remember feeling this wanted,' cracked Denman. The dinner jacket clearly brought out a different persona, one that knew how to play to a crowd.

'So what do you hope happens in June, Mr. Denman?' asked Doris, tucking her napkin in her lap. 'We can't have this communist Lumumba in charge?'

'Honey, we don't need to go there quite yet,' answered her husband, irritated that the conversation was going this way so early in the evening. The soup had just been served.

'It's all anyone can talk about, Harold,' added Libellule, 'you know that. Every party we go to, it's the same question: What will Lumumba do?'

'I'm not sure that is something that we can either control or get too worked up about,' Biver answered.

'Here, here,' said Count d'Aspremont, raising a glass to his host.

'Revolutions do not happen overnight,' said Reader. 'Look

at Algeria. Five years later, over a million dead and no functioning government. Would South Africa have done as well since the war if the blacks were in charge? I don't think so.'

'Oh, Timothy,' Beryl called. 'We can hear you down here. Not everyone shares your racist views, you know.'

Reader looked down the table, cocked his head and glared, before forking a tender loin of water buffalo into his mouth. Penderel noticed the sheepish expression her husband's gaze brought to Beryl's face. 'What I say is true,' he continued. 'And Congo will be a basket case for the next fifty years if these kaffirs get in charge.' Reader poured himself some wine, then topped off both Doris' and Libellule's glasses.

'Oh honey, it looks like we need more wine,' Beryl said, ringing the bell a little too loudly, before dropping her napkin on the floor.

'Some of us do … and some of us *clearly do not*,' Reader answered angrily. 'Darling, perhaps it's time for you to lie down? You've had a big day.'

'Dammit, I'm *fine*,' she said, slightly too emphatically.

'Let's go.'

'I said I'm fine.'

'Darling, I'll help you to the bedroom,' Reader reiterated, walking towards his wife. He grabbed her upper arm and Penderel could see his tight grip was hurting her. 'I'll be back in a minute. Jean-Pierre, please show our American guests the telescope. Perhaps we can even spot one of their U-2 planes overhead?'

The assembled guests watched silently, as the Readers walked towards the rear master bedroom. Denman looked over at Penderel, expressionless, as every one arose and headed outside.

'So you were in Brussels before coming here?' asked d'Aspremont. 'Brussels is a wonderful place. The heart of European civilization.'

Denman smiled. 'Yes, we liked living in Brussels very much, but I expect the French and Italians might disagree. Europe is such a disconnected collection of cultures. It's hard to say it has 'one heart.' Many hearts, many remain broken. The war wounds are still healing.'

'You're quite poetic, George, and quite correct. Europe in many ways is like the Belgian Congo. Different tribes, different histories, different geographies,' answered d'Aspremont, enjoying his cigar and snifter of brandy.

Reader returned to the verandah. Despite the evening coolness, he was sweating, his large sunburned face, bright red and dripping. His dinner jacket was unbuttoned, showing off an aging wrestler's physique, padded with fat. His shirt was untucked in the rear.

'Our hostess is well and sound asleep,' he said tersely. 'A little overserved today. Who needs another? I sure do.'

'So you fought in Tanganyika against the Germans for his Majesty?' Penderel asked Reader, as he returned with a full snifter of brandy. 'I too fought for the King. In the RAF. I was a tailgunner.'

'That *is* odd for a Yank,' Reader answered. 'And dangerous. You must have been quite young.'

'Yes, nineteen,' answered Penderel. 'I was in search of adventure. My mother was Kenyan. Grandparents had a coffee plantation up in the Aberdares. Never could make any money at it.'

'I didn't know that,' said Reader. 'You've come up a notch in my book.'

'Well, I'm off to bed myself,' said Penderel. 'We began the day at 5 a.m. in Leo. I think my colleague tucked himself in a little while ago and I should follow his example. He's my boss, after all. Good night, Timothy. I look forward to tomorrow.'

'Bring your tailgunner eye.'

'Good morning,' said Penderel. 'Thank you for a wonderful evening.' Penderel looked around the library. The dark teak furniture was shiny in the morning sun, as were the mangrove wood floors covered by gaily-colored Moroccan rugs. Beryl was already up, dressed for the day, drinking coffee alone.

She turned toward him, slow and reserved, with a sad smile.

'Are you all right?'

'Oh, yes, I'm fine,' she answered. 'Just had a little fall last night getting ready for bed. I may have had a touch too much to drink.'

Penderel looked right into her face and saw a purple shiner under her right eye and a cut on her mouth. 'Are you all right?'

'I'll be fine. Would you like some coffee?'

'Sure. I'll get it.'

Penderel looked out of the kitchen and saw Reader talking with several of the staff, as they were carrying provisions to the Land Rovers. He became instantly angry. He knew it wasn't a fall that gave her the black eye and split lip. She knew that he knew, but the weekend had to go on.

At that moment, Denman walked into the kitchen, smoking a cigarette. He no longer looked like Humphrey Bogart; he was back to playing the role of an accountant in awkward-fitting clothes. The brown, canvas hunting jacket was a size too big and the pleated wool pants swallowed up his slight lower body. 'Good morning, Dicky. Sleep well?'

'Better than our hostess, I'm afraid. Did you see the shiner?'

'Yes, I did,' Denman answered. 'It's none of our business.' He glanced out of the window at the preparations. 'Let's show these great white hunters that we can hold our own. Concentrate on the big game and forget about the bird with the shiny eye.'

The three Rovers set out toward the rear fields across the wooden bridge over the creek in front of the foothills. The cool morning air felt good on Penderel's face, yet he couldn't stop thinking about Beryl. *What kind of a man hits his wife?* He was twice her size. He likely swatted her with one of his beefy hands and knocked her into a wall or a sharp piece of furniture. He hated bullies. And men who beat women were the worst kind of bullies.

He thought about his father. Though Donald Penderel never physically hit his mother, he inflicted a short lifetime of pain onto her. Helen Penderel was only 34 when she died. Bed-ridden, asleep most of her adult life, prone to falling down and getting black eyes. What kind of life was that?

His mother spent most of her days shuttling between the bedroom, sewing room, dressing room, studio and bathroom. She spiked her milk with brandy and trudged around the upstairs in her slippers, sipping 'milk punch' as she called it. She tried her hand at painting and crocheting, but never had the willpower to finish anything. Occasionally the help would get her bathed and dressed for meals. And on a rare occasion, take her out for a drive in the Packard.

His father was the SOCONY representative to the Allied Petroleum Board in the 1930s, so he spent weeks away on long trips overseas. When he came home, he mostly yelled at his wife. *Clean yourself up! Eat something! You look too thin! Get outside! Have you spent any time with the boy? You look sickly!* Then he would leave again for another month, usually to Europe.

There was trouble brewing again in Germany. The war reparations from the Great War had turned Germany fearful and irrational. And oil would be the one commodity that the new Nazi party needed to gain their dominance of the continent.

Penderel hated his father for his absences, self-involvement and indifference. But most of all, he hated his father for what he did to his mother. A spirited, adventuresome woman transformed into a pathetic housebound drunk. *I really hate bullies*, Penderel thought to himself, as the Land Rover came across a swale and hit a bump, startling Penderel.

The three vehicles began to climb a short hill. One of the trackers who had been sent ahead on foot stood at the top of the rise with binoculars. He motioned to the driver, trotted down the hill, and whispered something to Reader.

'There's a large Roan buck about 500 meters out to our right, my eagle-eyed friend tells me,' said Reader. 'Mr. Penderel, as our guest, would you like to take the first shot? We may need to get a little closer.'

Penderel took one of the Winchester M-70s from the gun rack and four .308 cartridges and followed the tracker to the crest of the hill. The other three slowly walked up the hill. Penderel looked into the sight and through the brown, dying grass could make out the lone buck on a rise, short of a wooded area. 'This is probably as good a look as I'll get.'

Penderel lay down prone on the ground, looked through the sight at the majestic animal, took a long, deep breath and squeezed the trigger gently. A loud retort followed with flocks of birds scattering into the sky. The antelope dropped instantly.

Reader looked out across the expanse at the downed antelope, instantly dead. 'That's one hell of a shot,' he said to Penderel. 'You must have hit him in the spinal column. You were almost a half-kilometer away.' He shook Penderel's hand, laughing. 'Well done.'

'That was pure luck,' Penderel answered, shocked at his success.

'I think we have you in the wrong department,' Denman chuckled. 'We should enlist you for Katanga.' Reader looked up sharply. An awkward silence fell over the group before d'Aspremont jumped in.

'My father brought down an eland from that distance once,' he injected. 'But he'd been at it for three days. You've bagged a trophy and it's not yet time for morning tea.'

'Well, I think it is a good time for morning tea,' winked Reader, as he pulled out a bottle of brandy. 'Here's to more good shots.'

The third vehicle roared out across the field with two trackers to pick up and dress the antelope. When they returned, the four men were standing beside the vehicles, snacking on samosas, peanuts and a bottle of Hennessey.

Reader smiled as they began to pack up the trucks to head further along the ridgeline. 'It looks to be at least 700 pounds. You hit him right in the spine. I've known several guys who could shoot like that. Old friends. Some fought in Europe, a few others in Algeria.'

'Timothy, I don't think we need to retell old war stories,' d'Aspremont added quickly. 'Lots of colorful characters abound in these parts.'

They proceeded several miles east, passing by several thickets that had grown along the depressions. 'Sometimes, you'll see leopards in those copses. Sneaky devils,' said

Reader, pointing to the tangled trees and vines.

Below them, an enormous herd of Thomson gazelles stood gazing up at the noise on the hill. Another large herd of blue wildebeasts grazed among them. They stopped and got out to survey the landscape. 'That's quite a sight down there,' Denman remarked.

'Yes, we're blessed,' said Reader. 'To be able to preserve habitats like this is the key to this continent's future. Building a tourism industry is essential for us. The Kenyans, Rhodesians and South Africans have begun to do it. We have enough animals and have the vision for game parks and protected areas.'

'The first national preserve was in the Belgian Congo, up in the Virunga Mountains in the northeast,' d'Aspremont chimed in. 'My distant cousin, the King, established the park in the mid-20s. T'was very farsighted of him. A model for this continent.'

'Well, see it while it lasts,' Reader warned. 'The kaffirs are already screwing it all up. They can't figure out how to farm, so they kill and eat the animals. We're trying to set it up the right way in the south. It's over in the Congo. Particularly if that nigger gets power,' he said, looking at Penderel and Denman. 'That's what you people call them, right?'

'Some people do,' said Denman. 'But things are changing in the U.S. too.'

Penderel looked away awkwardly. *This guy is a monster.* He'd just added wife beater and blatant racist to this growing list.

After lunch, they packed up the vehicles and headed south along another open track. The afternoon sun began to cast shadows along the treeline. Up ahead, the first Land Rover suddenly stopped. Reader grabbed the binoculars, put them to his eyes and studied the eastern horizon. The driver gestured and pointed his finger along a line.

'We'll need to get closer. It's an eland. You practically need a bazooka to knock him down. He's a bull too. Mr. Denman, it's your turn. You have quite a tough act to follow.'

Denman could see a large, indistinct mass moving slowly in the distance. How anyone could tell it was an eland … or a Cape buffalo was beyond him. The patient tracker slowly demonstrated the shooting sequence for Denman. He nodded, repeated the steps, aimed and pulled the trigger. The eland was moving slowly towards him and Denman heard a throaty shriek.

'You hit him,' the tracker said. 'Looks like you shot him in the leg. He's still moving. Let's get closer.' Denman and the tracker roared ahead 100 meters in the Land Rover. The eland was wounded. 'We need to finish him off. Otherwise a lion or leopard will.'

Denman jumped out of the truck and fell to his knees

in the prone position and steadied the butt of the rifle against his shoulder. Deep breath, aim and fire. The eland went down instantly.

'Great shot,' said Reader. 'Rare anyone can drop an eland in one shot. Bulls can weigh almost a ton. Well done. You Americans are quite the sure shots.'

'We'll need to get Leon Tucci down soon,' said Reader. 'We like to get to know our American friends.'

After field-dressing the gigantic eland, the towed trailer on the third vehicle was riding low along the dirt road back towards Elysium. The men were tired and slightly tipsy from the constant flow of brandy through the early afternoon. They turned left past the thicket and just below was a female leopard walking alone toward the creek.

'OK, Harold and Jean-Pierre, who's up next?' Reader whispered. 'Bagging a leopard would make this a special day.'

D'Aspremont had fallen asleep, bouncing along the road. 'Clearly not our Count over here,' Biver laughed. 'I'm going to take a pass. I've killed too many animals already. My office looks like a taxidermist's. You take it, Timothy.'

Reader jumped out of the vehicle excitedly. He'd only killed one leopard and that was twenty years ago. 'Better go quickly before he runs away,' warned Biver.

Reader stood erect, aimed the rifle, clicked off the safety and pulled the trigger. *PACK-punk*, echoed through the swale.

'Shit, I missed,' he screamed. 'I fucking missed from this close!'

Birds scattered into the darkening blue sky and the leopard vanished into the thick brush.

'Well, we have enough meat to feed the staff for weeks,' Reader announced, walking up to the veranda as the outside lanterns were being lit. The three ladies were sitting around the table, sipping wine and smoking. In the tricky light, Beryl looked beautiful, Penderel thought. Makeup can hide any number of sins.

'Our new American friends showed us how the West was won. Mr. Penderel shot a 700-pound roan and Mr. Denman bagged an eland. And your poor husband missed a leopard from close in.'

'I'm so sorry, dear,' Beryl answered. 'But we need to save them for the tourists you want to bring here.'

After dinner, the group adjourned to the veranda for coffee. Reader was eager to give everyone a turn at the telescope, eagerly pointing out the different constellations. Count Harold d'Aspremont Lynden had turned in for the evening, the victim of too many mid-afternoon brandies, as had Libellule Biver. Penderel too was tired and looked forward to turning in soon. Tomorrow would be a long day flying back to Léopoldville and he needed a hangover like a set of barbells banging against his head.

'George, I'd like to get you back for another trip before the election,' Reader said, sipping a dram of Glenfiddich.

'We're all concerned about the election,' said Denman, 'but it's hard to imagine anything bad happening here. This really is heaven.'

Beryl turned, waving goodbye to the assembled group on the patio. 'I'm afraid I'm going to turn in. Don't stay up too late!' She turned and walked toward the library that led back to the master bedroom.

Penderel watched as she turned and disappeared around the corner. He returned to the veranda and began talking with Denman and Reader. He never remembered seeing Denman so animated and up this late.

'Your colleague and I were just remarking on your marksmanship skills,' said Reader, sipping freshly poured single malt. 'Dropping a 700-pound Roan from a half-kilometer is impressive.'

'Just beginner's luck,' said Penderel.

'I'm still impressed,' Reader answered, nodding. 'You

have a good eye and steady hands. I told George here that we should get your out in the field more. Tell me about your RAF days? I know shooting at airplanes coming at you in twenty below weather isn't easy.'

'Well,' Penderel remarked. 'With a turret-mounted machinegun, it's less aiming than you would think. It's more about leg cramps and not freezing your ass off.'

Denman too had poured another drink. 'And you know, he was decorated by King George. And on his last mission in Korea for our side, he nearly didn't make it.'

Penderel looked up shyly. He'd never heard Denman go on about anything, particularly personal praise. He was clearly tight, but comfortable with Timothy Reader. Funny he thought. *Odd bedfellows.*

'After the war, I went back to the States, but realized a desk job was not ever going to work for me,' Penderel said. 'So I reenlisted in the U.S. Air Force and went to Korea. I must be a sucker for punishment, I guess. We'd just finished a bombing run over the Yalu River and were headed back to Okinawa. We'd hit a bridge and supply convoy. Just as we were climbing out over the Yellow Sea, three MiGs bounced us. Rounds hit the wing tanks. We all had to bail out. I figured my number was finally up. We all got out, but the pilot's chute didn't open.'

Denman looked over at Penderel with pride. 'That's quite a story. But you survived,' Reader said, turning to pour more scotch into his glass. Denman followed suit.

'Yeah,' Penderel answered. 'I hit the water. It was cold, but it was summertime. The co-pilot got tangled up in his chute and drowned. It still haunts me,' Penderel said, finishing his drink. 'I think I'd better get to bed.'

Penderel took leave toward the library and turned to see his boss and Reader laughing, like old friends.

He saw a light on in the bathroom past his bedroom and crept silently toward it. The door was ajar and the water was running. He could see Beryl looking into a mirror. She turned her head to one side, then to the other. She raised her forehead and looked down her nose, blinking her eyes. She was standing in a nightgown and robe, shifting positions, making faces, raising and lowering her mouth. First pouty, then she flared her nostrils like a confident actress preparing to go on stage. She exercised her mouth and stretched her chin. She pulled her blond hair up with her hands; then she tousled it, shaking her head sassily.

Penderel watched in amazement at this woman in front of a mirror, knowing he should leave. But he was fascinated by her rituals of self-examination. Was it vanity? Maybe she just enjoyed altering the image of herself, fantasizing she was someone else? Even with the bruise, Beryl Reader was still a beautiful middle-aged woman, sadly relegated to observing that herself. It made him mad. She deserved better than that monster of a husband.

He quietly slipped down the hallway to the guest room.

He heard a sound. Beryl had followed him down the hallway.

'Do you always spy on your hosts? It must be a genetic thing with you people.' But Beryl was teasing. She approached quickly and quietly, extending her neck and face for a kiss. 'I saw you in the mirror. You're not much of a spy, after all.'

Penderel took her in his arms, pleased by her muscular build. She had the form of a rider, taut, thick yet lanquid, athletic and smooth. She pulled him close, the smell of Vol de Nuit and Yardley's lavender soap immediately came through his nostrils, exciting, but relaxing him. She stared at him, ugly shiner displayed honestly.

'You will come back before the election?' she asked softly, pulling away.

'I promise, Beryl, I promise.'

Nine

March 1960

'George,' Penderel asked as he walked into Denman's office. 'I need to get out of Leo to see what's going on. It's an echo chamber in here.'

'I agree. We're just picking up the Belgians' scraps. What's your idea?'

'Well, Justin-Marie Bomboko asked that I come up to Colquilhatville. Probably can figure out more from going there than sitting here talking to scared Belgians and gossip-prone shopkeepers and restauranteurs. I'd like to take a ferry just to see what this place looks like from the ground.'

Denman smiled, nodding, tamping down his unlit cigarette. 'When do you go?'

Penderel boarded the enormous double-deck, paddle steamer in Maluku. It looked like an old Mississippi riverboat dragged out of comfortable retirement in Mobile Bay and put to overwork and humiliation on the Congo River. The state-run river transport agency called OTRACO had refurbished it somewhat, but the vessel was rusty and run-down. Parts of it were painted deep orange to match the rust. He smiled at the handpainted white letters along the bow: DELIVERANCE.

Penderel had a small cabin that consisted of a wooden-slatted bed, a stained mattress and a flimsy metal chair. It looked to have been recently painted with a wet mop and the small porthole was sealed shut. At least the mosquitos couldn't get in.

The tiny sink basin and the toilet were dirty, water-stained and smelled badly of the last occupant. Even in the dappled morning sun, the heat and droning of insects was deafening. The first class cabins were attached to the wheelhouse at the bow of the boat.

Behind the steamer sat two large open barges, lashed together with a cobweb of thick rope. This was third class. A kaleidoscope of different shapes, sizes and smells lay out behind him, as passengers staked their real estate and began constructing their temporary residence. In many ways, this was a floating marketplace. Vendors were setting up small stalls covered with canvas awnings. There was an echoing of hammers and the laughter of people excited for a long trip ahead and profits to be made.

Most of the passengers were women, who had carried car-sized bundles on their shoulders through the maze and boobytraps of humanity. Cages of domesticated poultry and the pungent fish sat drying on sun-heated surfaces. Privacy was non-existent. On the journey, people would shit, eat, bathe, sleep and tell stories. It was both communal and impersonal – the pillars of poverty.

A burly, bearded sweat-soaked man came through the doorway by the wheelhouse carrying a large pack. He had several smaller cases flung across his shoulder. 'Hello,' he said softly, poking his head inside the cabin door. 'Hello. Teddy Pulman. Seems like we'll be neighbors.'

'Hi, the name's Richard.'

Just then, a thin, wiry man, who looked to be in his mid-forties, trudged along the deck and poked his head in. 'Bon jour,' he said.

'Hello Frank,' said Pulman. 'Glad you made it. This is Richard …'

'Richard Penderel,' sticking out his hand. 'Good morning.'

'This is my colleague, Frank Quadflieg from the Léopoldville Zoo. He's going all the way to the far northeast with me.'

'How far is all the way?'

'Well, we head to Bumba on this boat where the river goes south. Then we take a train toward Goma. Then a taxicab and a few ox carts. It will take us two weeks if we're lucky.'

The engines had been turned on, so the smell of diesel fuel and smoke had begun to permeate the cabins.

'Well, at least there is a boat,' Quadflieg said. 'And we look to be close to schedule,' he continued, checking his watch.

Penderel smiled. He liked their calm and nonchalance. Clearly they knew the territory.

'I'm headed to Coq to visit a friend.'

'Justin-Marie Bomboko?' asked Quadflieg.

Penderel nodded. 'I guess I don't look like a missionary.'

'He's a good man. One of the few who has a clue of what's going on. He's the UNIMO candidate. A Mongo chief, I believe. These poor people need all the advice they can get. My countrymen have been useless in preparing them.'

The horn sounded as the water around the boat began to churn. 'Here we go.' Teddy pulled a pint of Cutty Sark out of his pack, took a long draught and passed it to Penderel. 'Here's to a safe trip.'

Penderel took two gulps, shivered and handed it to the other zookeeper, who raised the bottle. 'Proost!'

Throngs of brightly colored people waved from the dock as the clunky steamer wheezed and tooted through the ovaltine-colored, oil-sheened water. The trio climbed the wooden ladder to the bridge and gazed out into the morning sun. The Congo River was an enormous lake, punctuated by sandbars, clumps of grass and small islands. The low-slung buildings of Brazzaville passed by on the port side.

The river was still, thick and shiny. Small dugout pirogues, overloaded with bundles of textiles crossed closely in front of the steamer, oblivious to the horns. Flat-bottomed skiffs carrying firewood ambled along the shoreline. Five lanky boys paddled a skinny twelve-foot canoe. An elderly woman holding a colorful umbrella was plopped down in the center, like a grand African queen. The wake of the steamer nearly tipped the canoe over. The captain laughed, waving.

'These are good people, these Congolese,' Quadflieg continued. 'Why didn't you fly? This will take a few days … if we're lucky.'

'Been here for four months and haven't seen the land up close. Have a few days off. Why not?'

'If you're patient and don't mind discomfort, it's the best way to see this country,' he continued. 'It was better five years ago. The Belgians have stopped putting money into the infrastructure.'

The Belgian captain came down the ladder and entered the cabin. He was short and muscular and pressed a firm handshake to his three first class passengers. 'Sorry about the tight accommodations. As you can see, third class fills up quickly.' They looked out over the expanse astern, as it continued to take shape, overladen with humanity and goods.

'This is quite the marketplace,' remarked Penderel. 'What are they trading?'

'Coming up river, it's city goods. Razor blades, batteries, pills, cigarettes, pencils, shoes, gramophone records, lengths of fabric, soap, you name it. Coming back, it's dried fish, dried bushmeat, fruits, and timber. This is the main highway for the country.'

'Bushmeat's part of the reason we're here,' Pulman jumped in. 'There's a growing problem with the natives eating endangered species. We're worried that if nothing's done, the forests will be depleted in twenty years. All the animals will be gone, poached or eaten.'

The captain looked down smiling sheepishly and nodding. 'Well, there are plenty of fish. I hope you like them, as it basically is our menu. Some manioc and stewed greens, maybe a pineapple or melon as we get upstream. You've seen your last baguette for a while. Get yourselves settled in and join us up in the wheelhouse. This part of the trip is nice. It can get a little rougher upstream.'

The wide rolling, cocoa river continued to cut through the tussocks of grasses, floating lily pads and thick beds of water hyacinth. Penderel wondered how many boats got entangled in the river here. It was swampy mire that smelled of vegetation, both alive and rotten. The grey sky reached down to meet the water, so the vista looked narrow and confined. Small boats would come out of the gloom, pass rapidly, and disappear again. It was though they were in a dream, images without context, with only the diesel engine sputtering along uninterrupted.

Penderel stood on the bridge with a cigarette, the orange tip glowing like a beacon. The two others sat in their cabins, reading and sorting out maps and sheathes of paper. It was quiet except for the lapping of the river along the side of the boat and the occasional laughter or high-pitched yell from the towed barges.

He could barely make out the figures on the barges, though it had the order of a scout camp, made of plastic, twine and misshapen sticks of wood. He could see the second-class passengers in front of him, hanging over the railings, pointing and giggling. For many of them, this was a first-class trip – a boat going upstream against the current that didn't have to be paddled.

Penderel headed below to the second-class deck. It had the same open plan, but these were people in transit. They weren't selling anything, instead heading for upriver towns and settlements. There were piles of bananas, live chickens and ducks tied together squawking and heaps of dried and smoked fish. The women washed their children from buckets that they lowered over the gunwale into the river. Some were preparing food on small cookstoves.

The men sat crouched in a circle smoking and talking. One man walked towards the group with a large plastic plate of smoked fish. His wife gestured angrily, likely having to do with his generosity and their collective idleness. There were mischievous monkeys bouncing around, yelling. The choreography and economy of movement amazed Penderel. No space was unoccupied, people weaved and accommodated, yet no one seemed to be agitated or cramped, except for lazy man's wife.

The wide river narrowed several hours upstream from Leo. The banks of the river rose and the current increased, putting a strain on the steady engine. Rocks replaced the water hyacinth and the large cluttered bathtub had finally become a river. Ahead along the horizon to the northwest, storm clouds were building. The monotone grey sky was turning purple. A sudden violent wind came up and the dense canopy of trees on the bank began to sway.

Penderel craned his head to check the telltales. Weather had always been the constant unknowable when flying, so monitoring it was his natural habit.

Huge raindrops suddenly turned the water in front of him to chaos. The thud of the rain on the tin roof of the cabin was deafening. Leaves on the trees began to pop and flutter helplessly. Penderel quickly climbed the ladder to the top deck and entered the wheelhouse. 'Need any help? Pretty bad storm brewing.'

'Sure,' said the captain. 'Can you work that spotlight for us? Need to know how far that bank is,' pointing starboard. It was almost six p.m., so the day's light was quickly fading. The thick vines and leaves glistened from the rain and reflection of the beamed light.

'Looks like ten meters,' he yelled. The captain turned the ship slightly toward the center of the river. The navigator called out depth calculations from the dimly lit chart room. The torrents of water kept coming without any let-up. Periodic bolts of lightning erupted across the sky like camera flashbulbs, illuminating the shape of the river.

'How are those people on the barge?' Penderel yelled over the splatter.

'They're fine,' the captain answered. 'We get one of these storms every afternoon. It cools everyone down.'

At this point, the two zoologists entered the wheelhouse, a shared plastic sheet over their heads. 'Quite a deluge.'

The captain yelled over the clanking of the rain, 'It'll be past us in ten minutes. Cleans out the skies and does away with sins. Our own little nautical Bible story we get every afternoon. Seems apropos, given your occupations.'

The storm passed and a clear moonlit night came over the river. The high-pitched songs from the trees became deafening, each insect trying to outshout the other. Penderel retired to his cabin. He adjusted the small light by the bed with the fraying cord, and he opened the book to the page he had folded over. The river was calm and he could barely hear the chorus outside.

'Going up that river was like travelling back to the earliest beginnings of the world, when vegetation rioted on the earth and the big trees were kings. The broadening waters flowed through a mob of wooded islands; you lost your way trying to find the channel, till you thought yourself bewitched and cut off forever from everything you had known once – somewhere -- far away in another existence perhaps. There were moments when one's past came back to one; but it came in the shape of an unrestful and noisy dream, remembered with wonder amongst the overwhelming realities of this strange world of plants, and water, and silence.

'A noisy dream, remembered with wonder,' he nodded, listening to this strange world of plants, and water, and silence. *Jesus, Joseph Conrad can really write*, he thought to himself, shutting the book. *And English wasn't even his first language!*

The land flattened and the river widened the next morning. The boat continued to chug along, occasionally sounding its horn to greet the great jungle. Every few miles there were little clearings alongside the river. No more than a dozen palm frond huts on stilts sat on the muddy bank.

In an instant, a flotilla of emissaries in small dugout canoes paddled furiously toward the steamer, timing their strokes and approach angles. The canoes were filled with fruit, maize, dried fish and dried red and grey monkeys splayed on sticks like a child's kite, awkwardly loaded wicker chairs, and large mortars carved out of tree trunks. Penderel couldn't figure out how anyone could control that much top-heavy weight and still manage to guide the vessel to the moving boat.

The docking process mid-river was intricate and choreographed. Lines were tossed from the barge and grabbed by the boys or girls in the canoes. These were tied to cleats on the flat steel barge. Occasionally the connection would be missed or the canoe would capsize from the wake of the steamer. Little was done or said if that occured. They would somehow get back to shore or be taken by a crocodile.

'The whites are all leaving the plantations up here,' Quadflieg said over lunch. The plump perch had been delicately cooked over a fire in the tiny, unlit first class kitchen. 'As are the missionaries.' Penderel had noticed abandoned stucco buildings along the shoreline and asked about life along the river.

'It's a shame,' added Pulman. 'Their forefathers enslaved the people, but this generation of whites tried to teach the natives about things like agriculture, building construction, infrastructure, using the land right. But they've packed up quickly and gone. In ten years, the jungle will reclaim this whole river.'

'What's your take on the future, Frank?' Penderel asked.

'I'm very discouraged. Everyone I know in Leo is leaving,' said Quadflieg. 'These dust-ups and protests have everyone scared. I don't blame them. The military has been the one institution that has kept the country a civil society. When mutinies start in the barracks over pay or control, it'll be something like that, then there will be chaos. I worry about our zoo. The animals will be slaughtered.'

'There's an enormous national park up in that area outside Goma we're headed to,' continued Quadflieg. 'It's the last refuge for mountain gorillas on the Uganda border. It's the one place we have hope for. Some of the mountains go up to 15,000 feet. There're active volcanoes, too. We're meeting two Americans – a husband and wife – who have been up there for the past year studying the gorillas.'

'Have you ever seen gorillas in the wild?' Penderel asked. 'Outside of the movie theatre?'

'Only once … from far away,' added Pulman. 'We were there last year and spotted a family of eight. It's amazing to watch. I'm so happy that someone is trying to understand them. Left to their devices, the Congolese will plow up their habitat and kill them.'

'We're in a race against time and humanity, Mr. Penderel,' Frank Quadflieg softly added. The heat, humidity and two days of travel had tired him out already. His face was florid and sweat soaked through his shirt. 'You should try to see them before you leave the country.'

The next morning the steamer pulled into the wharf at 7:45 a.m., exactly 48 hours after leaving the capital. 'Welcome to Coquilhatville, the capital of the Équateur Province,' the captain announced. The sun had come up over the trees. It was a beautiful, warm morning and Penderel could see Justin-Marie Bomboko waving on the dock. A group of people surrounded him, cheering.

Quadflieg looked up. 'I guess there is a political campaign going on.' Bomboko had positioned himself right by the gangway to wave and shake hands with those disembarking from first and second class. Those on the barge had their own exitway, across a mud flat. Bomboko didn't seem focused on them.

'My dear friend Richard,' Bomboko approached Penderel, 'Welcome to Coq. I'm so happy you are here.'

'Jean-Marie, this is Frank Quadflieg and Teddy Pulman. They're zoologists.'

'Mr. Quadflieg and I have met a few times. Wildlife conservation is an important issue facing our country. Would you care to join me for a celebratory cocktail at our well-known café that straddles the Equator? It's a little early, but that way we can toast one another in both hemispheres at the same time.'

'Of course.'

Later that day, Bomboko and Penderel sat down alone in his villa outside of town after their drink at the Oasis, followed by a short tour of town and lunch. There was a small U.N. outpost with two employees, a disused factory, a toppled stone that Stanley placed near the southern riverbank and a ten-story city hall building still under construction with a statue of Leopold II on top. There were foundations for a bridge across the river to connect to French Congo, which were now grown over and crumbling back into the jungle. Like Léopoldville, it was a city with a grand, impractical vision that would never be realized.

'Do you see our plight?' Bomboko asked. 'Usually there is excitement and energy around independence. Things are being built; there's investment in the future. Throughout Congo, it is the opposite. I despair that this will be a disaster.'

'The United States will help you,' Penderel answered. 'This country needs to steer a moderate course to succeed. There is concern that you will follow the more radical socialist pan-African path posited by Nkrumah. Is that true?'

'Our country is very divided. Lumumba is the only one running a national campaign – but the people of Leo and

Elisabethville will never vote for him. The Belgians might be right. One hundred years may still not be enough for us.'

'We've talked last week about forming a coalition with the other parties. What allies to you have?'

'Kasazubu, Adoula, Ileo, Kalonji are the main ones, the pragmatic ones. Tshombe? Probably, though he is a difficult, hardheaded man. Lumumba and Gizenga are the opposition.'

'Yes, Tshombe is hardheaded,' Penderel answered. 'But he wants stability more than anything else. He'll continue to push for Belgian support.'

'We all need Belgian support,' Bomboko continued soberly, shaking his head. 'But what we really need is the U.S.'

'How about the army guy? Mobutu?' Penderel asked. He was the invisible presence. 'Is he close to Lumumba?'

'Joseph Mobutu. He's an ambitious man. I've known him for years. He's been wise to align himself with Lumumba, but he has higher goals. I believe he can be an ally of ours. It might take awhile.'

'Justin-Marie, we're prepared to help you. That needs to be quietly communicated to those that you trust.'

'Thank you, Richard.'

Ten

April 1960

Penderel was sitting in the consulate reviewing Bomboko's requests for money. When he offered support, he didn't realize it would be so expensive. He trusted Bomboko more than the others, though Victor Nendaka was also a quietly powerful presence. He was the taciturn skeptic to Bomboko's cheerful front man.

The phone rang. 'Hello.'

'Hello, Richard, this is Beryl Reader.'

'Hello, Beryl,' Penderel answered, relaxing, sliding back in his chair. The last time he'd seen her they embraced in a hallway. Still it was a clear and memorable and he'd replayed the event many times since. 'So good to hear from you again.'

There was a short silence, then an uneasy laugh. 'Well, I

happen to be in Léopoldville today and wanted to know if you were available for lunch?'

'Yes, of course.' He tried to sound calm, but knew his excitement was audible. His mind quickly raced to a passionate rendezvous. *She's calling me out of the blue. For what reason?* 'How about the café in the Memling?'

'That would be perfect. How's one o'clock? I have a meeting over at the university that should finish up by then.'

Denman overheard the call. There was little privacy in the small consulate. He came over and smiled after Penderel hung up.

'I told you to be careful with that bird. We've had our eye on her. She comes to Leo monthly for meetings at the university. But she spends time with an assortment of people while she is here -- politicians, business people, Belgians. Keep your wits about you and watch what you say. I saw the looks between you. And you know the deal with her husband.'

Beryl Reader was sitting at the bar at the hotel, sipping a cup of coffee, as Penderel walked in. She wore a tailored, khaki-colored linen dress. Her blond hair was pulled back and she wore bright red lipstick. The marks from six weeks back had vanished.

He didn't know what to expect since their last meeting,

but she looked somewhat more formal than he'd anticipated. He had recurrent visions of checking into one of the Memling's finest suites on his walk over from the consulate. She quickly jumped into the familiar subject of the elections scheduled in six weeks.

'Well, we discussed this before and my opinions haven't changed much,' Penderel began dejectedly. He paused and exhaled. 'I liken it to betting on horses in their first race. Lumumba is the best speaker and motivator, but he's inconsistent. He's the show pony with the bright tack and high-stepping flair. Then there's Kasavubu, dull but competent. He's more of a workhorse, probably better pulling a plow up and down a field than running around a racetrack.

'Your man Tshombe is the hard one to read – at times supportive of independence, other times hesitant,' Penderel continued, hoping that this was not the real reason for her call. Opining about the election using different metaphors had been the singular topic over the past month. 'He's the dark horse, if you don't mind my analogy. Then there are the local players being put in to round out the field. But it's a weak field, I'm afraid. They'll get better with practice.'

Penderel felt like a trite raceway tout, hoping the conversation would get more personal.

'Who are you betting on?' She flashed a smile, as the cigarette smoke curled up into the dark wooden rafters of the bar.

'We don't get to vote,' said Penderel. 'How about you? What's your prediction?'

'A bloody civil war that will last fifty years. That's what I'm goddamned afraid of!' Beryl said, voice bursting with anger and emotion. She suddenly looked small, sad and completely sincere. She tried to smile after her outburst.

'C'mon. *Really?* You're not a pessimist,' Penderel answered, off-footed. He'd observed opposite Beryls in the course of ten minutes: confident, flirtatious Beryl, then honest, scared Beryl. 'Don't you believe that this country will succeed? It has land, abundant natural resources. It sits in the heart of Africa. The Congo can lead this continent forward.' He hoped a positive outlook would improve her mood.

'You Americans are optimists,' Beryl answered slowly. 'I like you because of that. No mountain you won't scale. No river you won't ford. I'm practical. I love this continent. It is my home. But the Europeans have a duty to actively transform it into a decent, open and free place. And they are not doing one goddamn thing, except robbing the bank – the mines that belong to the Congolese people!' Her face was drained and her jaw jutted out. She took a deep breath and sat back in the chair.

'I apologize for being so emotional, but I just had a long and frustrating meeting,' she continued, fiddling for a cigarette in her clutch. Penderel leaned forward and offered her a light. 'The politics of academia! The challenge to get this country prepared and educated for the future scares me. Twenty college graduates a year is pathetic! There are fourteen million people here. What the Belgians did here was criminal!'

'I understand. We're all frustrated and worried about what will happen,' said Penderel, watching his hope for an afternoon fling go sideways.

Beryl stood up from the table unsteadily. She had become ashen. They had not even ordered lunch yet and she'd smoked two cigarettes and had only one sip of wine. 'I apologize, but I'm going to have to leave now. I'm not feeling well.' Her voice was quivering and she swallowed after each sentence. 'I'm sorry.'

She put her clutch under her arm and walked out of the restaurant. She didn't look back.

Penderel sat down to finish his glass of wine, muddling over the uneven flying patterns of *that bird.* Was she sincere? She looked it, but she had a thespian's flair to dominate any moment she desired. Who upset her today? A bunch of white geology professors preparing to skip town? Had she met with other Belgians in power? She seemed to dislike them. But she was thick as thieves with the UMHK.

He paid his bill and trudged back to the consulate, hungry and horny.

Eleven

May 1960

The anxiety in Léopoldville rose with the humidity as the elections loomed. Each day, a little more of the old order flagged, as tempers frayed and people -- black and white -- began to worry about their futures. There were rumors that 800 kilos of mail had been found stuffed down the post office drains. Delvaux's neighbors had been robbed twice. The first incident was a set of sun curtains that were cut down before the thief heard voices upstairs and ran away. Next came the robbery of a brand new set of bath towels from the clothesline in the middle of the afternoon.

Then there was the story of the Turk who ran the best fabric shop in town. One evening, hearing noises downstairs in the store, he grabbed his rifle and shot the young thief in the back as he jumped through the window, bolt of Egyptian linen in his arms. Getting killed over a fancy bolt of fabric? The police arrested the Turk, but let him off when they realized the thief was just some dumb Lulua.

Penderel heard an amusing story at the men's club in town. Two enterprising women planned to open a 'charm school' for the spouses of the rising black politicians. For a small fee, they could become 'ladies' overnight, certificates included. The spouses would be taught a range of hostess skills, including how to set a table, prepare a menu, conduct social comportment, establish dress codes, and make general small talk.

The expat gossip mill was aghast. How on earth could two wives of mid-level civil servants from Liege *of all places* pull such a venture off? Drinks were ordered to discuss this more.

Penderel's operative, Habib Khouri, told Penderel he believed that tribal clashes were the real problem, though they were rarely reported. In Leo, the Byakkas and the Abakos had been skirmishing over the past few months, leaving behind scores of machete wounds and missing hands. The military came in and tried to break the fights up. This would last until the following evening, when the same groups would get into the beer and dope and do it all over again.

Last week, a fight between the Luluas and the Balubas over in Leo II Belge closed down the market. The police and the military responded, until they got distracted and started shouting over which group had jurisdiction. Order was finally restored when the Belgian troops arrived.

Penderel thought it odd that most of the Belgian expats enjoyed the worldwide attention they received every day in their huge continental backwater, when all it did was show the world what inept colonists they had been. Sadly, the planeloads of the arriving press barely knew the first thing about the Belgian Congo. One in particular – a young American freelancer recently graduated from Yale – even asked how the French planned to handle the turnover.

At a British Embassy barbecue, one of the founders of the charm school venture became sexually aroused when Geoff Peters from *The Daily Express* asked her opinion on the future of Congo. She appeared to swoon when discussing the magnetism of Patrice Lumumba. At least that's what Delvaux quipped to Penderel.

'This isn't going to go well,' Habib said. It was a sunny Saturday afternoon in the middle of May. Purveyors of vegetables and seafood had paraded through the restaurant, while Habib dispatched orders to the kitchen staff in Lingala for the busy upcoming evening. Le Restaurant Cedars Élevé was booked solid from 6 to 9:30.

Penderel looked up from a plate of cheese and a glass of sherry. The waitstaff was beginning to set up for the evening. The clanking of glasses and cutlery and happy exchanges pinged through the door to the kitchen. Everyone was looking forward to another big night. 'How so?'

Habib peered over to Penderel, who was taking a deep drag of a cigarette. Habib was a smart, practical man, who trusted everyone and no one equally. He was small and energetic with neatly trimmed graying hair and a rich, expressive moustache that veiled his fears and disappointments. The last month had been extremely busy at the restaurant with most of his patrons, most nights, staying late, stumbling out of the restaurant drunk. But the mood was less about happy, contented celebration than fear of what was to come. The panic had set in.

'People are scared,' Habib began. 'Really scared. Many of the Belgians are trying to get out, others are walling themselves in for the final fight.' Habib stared at Penderel. 'Then there are the Soviets.'

'Go on,' Penderel motioned. The nicotine on top of the sherry and grim prognosis made him anxious.

'There was a table of Greeks talking away last night. They were throwing around plenty of money, which Greeks here don't have. I overheard a conversation about an arms shipment that landed in Dar es Salaam last week. Assume it's the Soviets.'

'Why?' asked Penderel. 'How do the Soviets benefit from starting a war? Don't they realize they can gain influence by not firing a shot? Lumumba is their man.'

'Meddling. Keeping the west off-footed,' said Habib.

'That's their goal. Then there is the other factor. I heard that mercenaries are coming in from the south. There's a blabby Belgian military guy who was in last week, too.'

'Help, me Habib,' answered Penderel, exhausted and confused. 'You know I rely on your instincts. Mercenaries? From where, who's bringing them in?'

'The Belgians, of course,' Habib began. 'It's mostly young white Africans in need of a job. The Begians will first bait Lumumba into making a dumb populist gesture -- say forcing the officer corps of the *Force Publique* to integrate. That will stir things up and give Katanga the pretext to break away. Then all hell will break loose. No one is ready for this. Except Tshombe. He's been ready for months. The Soviets are the least of the problems.'

'How do you know all this?' Penderel's mind was reeling. Habib was able to craft a narrative out of a combination of facts, conversations and rumors. Penderel wished he had that gift.

'I don't,' Habib replied. 'Some of this is common sense. People do reckless things on the eve of the unknown. The arms shipments and flood of mercenaries is the beginning of a civil war.'

'Habib,' Penderel answered. 'Time to get you and your family out of here.'

'No, I will not leave,' he answered. 'But I want you to get my wife and children to Brazzaville if things go badly.

That was our agreement.'

'Indeed it was,' answered Penderel. 'And I will.'

Over his eight-and-a-half months in country, Penderel had taken in the human stories of an unprepared place in the midst of change. He saw the cynicism of the colonial dames starting a business now. He had watched the upending of the eighty-year social order, which made the remaining white colonials even more eccentric and desperate. And now, the Soviet Union had begun its meddling and a civil war was about to start.

The urgent issue was what would happen to the fifteen million people who had to stay? Elections were next week. In five weeks, everything would change and charm school would be a distant consideration.

He was headed to Elisabethville next week to have a chat with Biver and meet the Chief of the Africa Division, Prescott Dillon. With the Katanga election in little doubt, he needed to think about contingency planning.

Twelve

Early June 1960

He loved visits to Elisabethville. The quiet sense of order and cool of the air appealed to him. It was so different from the hurly-burly of Leo and its unending list of problems and dramas. This was his fourth visit, including the weekend in February at Elysium. He learned a little more on each trip, but this was a kept town with very few reliable listening posts.

Recently, he had confirmation of Habib's tip that several military guys were in Katanga, somewhere outside of town. The names Mike Hoare and Frenchman Bob Denard came up. He knew them by reputation as soldiers of fortune, both World War II veterans. Denard was a recent participant in the Algerian conflict. Hoare was a Durban-based Irishman who ran safaris. They were not to be messed with, but it was important that he knew where they were and what they were up to.

Penderel felt Timothy Reader had to be connected, though he clung to the 'commercial relations' job description. There were further rumors that gangs of white Africans were preparing to get into the fray for whomever paid the best. Penderel knew the last thing the U.S. wanted was a private army marauding around this new country, further destabilizing what was likely to be a mess.

What Penderel enjoyed most about coming to Elisabethville was spending time with Beryl. It was always over social interactions within a larger group that included Biver and Beryl's husband, but she was reliably flirtatious. She was back in form after that odd episode in Leo the prior month. Penderel missed female company.

'So Dicky,' Beryl said after lunch, sipping a cup of coffee. 'I like the name Dicky. Masculine, but informal. What do I hear about you being a war hero?' Her husband and Biver had returned to their offices and Penderel was killing time until his 3 p.m. rendezvous with the new chief of the Africa Division who was passing through Elisabethville.

'All rumors, none true,' he answered playfully.

'You were a tailgunner in the RAF and later in the U.S. Air Force. Right?'

Penderel nodded slowly. Denman had strangely brought that subject up one late night in March at Elysium.

'Did you really tell a reporter from the *Stars and Stripes* that you'd rather fly combat missions than date Marilyn Monroe?'

'Let's say I don't feel that way any longer,' he chuckled, lighting a cigarette, offering one to Beryl. 'Ah, the arrogance of youth!'

'You were only one of three Yanks awarded a Distinguished Service Medal by His Majesty, the King of England? My husband mentioned that.' Beryl put her hand over his to steady the lighter. She puffed and sat back in her chair.

'Sadly, right again. We lost a lot of people in that war. I was lucky to survive. You have quite a dossier on me!' He flicked his lighter shut and put it in his pocket.

'And then you volunteered to go to Korea and got shot down over the Yellow Sea? Followed by a Medal of Honor from your President Truman? Seems you're a glutton for adventure? Or medals?'

'No one has ever put my life story in that few questions. I never thought it could be that dull. I'm just a patriot,' he answered. 'And you? You're just a geologist? You must be more interesting than that. I'd say you're a forensic historian.'

'Oh, the false modesty of a reluctant hero! Pullease! All of us white Africans need to have a range of skills. No one can afford to be too specialized. They're too few of us. Your story didn't require much digging. But count me as impressed. Tshombe surely was.'

Penderel laughed uncomfortably. He didn't like his past being such a known quantity. He was supposedly a spy, after all. 'What do you and Timothy do with your free time? You don't have children, do you?' He hoped turning the subject to her husband would shake something loose.

'No we don't. Considered it, but things just didn't work out.' She took a quick drag of her cigarette, leaning forward. 'And you?' she asked. 'You don't strike me as the marrying type.'

'I wasn't. Never could find the right girl. Guess I was too busy.'

'Avoiding Marilyn Monroe no doubt,' Beryl said, 'or collecting medals.' She stubbed her cigarette out. 'You really should take in this magnificent country before it goes to hell. I believe I mentioned it, but the Albert National Park outside Goma is terrific. Go see the gorillas. They're remarkable creatures. Hollywood ruined what people think of them. Helping protect them is one of the few things the Belgians did right.'

'I'll need a guide.'

'Tempting invitation,' she answered. 'Perhaps I'll consider it.'

Penderel blushed as she stood up and shook his hand firmly. She sashayed out into the bright, clear afternoon.

'Could I have a whiskey?' he called to the bartender, looking at his watch. The CIA's Africa head, Prescott Dillon wasn't due for another half-hour. He had been with the agency for fourteen years and had served in various African countries since his arrival in 1954.

Dillon had refereed the Mau Mau uprising with the Brits, helped head off the Suez Crisis in 1956, warily watched the Algerian and Sudanese civil wars and helped shepherd peaceful independence movements in Tunisia, Ghana, Senegal, Guinea, Togo and Cameroon over the past five months.

Dillon was reportedly brilliant, but also arrogant and hyper-political. This was a common description of nearly everyone Penderel had met. 'Be careful exactly what you tell him or we'll have Allen Dulles crawling up our assholes,' Denman had warned.

After he finished his drink, Penderel retreated to the hotel lobby. Better to be seen there by your superior officer than in a bar at three in the afternoon. *Let him decide where we sit to talk*, he thought to himself. A small, fast-walking man came through the empty lobby at 2:55. They exchanged introductions, shook hands briskly and turned to head back to the bar.

'Pretty interesting time to be here,' Dillon remarked as they were seated at a table in the rear of the empty room. 'You been here for eight months now?'

'Yes sir, it's been quite an experience. It's my first

overseas posting. Something seems to shift every day here.'

'Indeed. Who knew this sleepy continent would *awake*? We need to be on the right side of these freedom movements. But we also need to control them. There's always tension between the practical and the political.'

'Yes, I understand.' Penderel watched carefully and tried to speak even more astutely. This was his big shot to show he belonged in the agency. He wasn't just a war hero that no one knew what to do with.

'Just came from Pretoria, off to Nairobi at five tonight. The South Africans are dug in for the long haul. Too bad, it will haunt them.' He looked up at Penderel. 'Where in the hell can I get a good drink with ice that won't make me sick?'

'Just a minute,' Penderel answered, motioning to the bartender. 'What would you like suh?'

'Black Label and purified ice, thank you.'

'Of course,' he smiled. 'Our ice is *always* purified.'

'What's your assessment so far?' Dillon continued, fiddling with a pen.

'It's complicated without a straight line or a straight partner to deal with yet,' Penderel began. He'd practiced this speech in the mirror. 'We're working on it. Lumumba is popular, but he isn't prepared to govern. Katanga is the exception.'

Penderel paused to take in Dillon's expression. He was slowly nodding, though his hands were busy with the ballpoint pen. 'He continued. 'There are rumblings that the province will secede. I suspect Tshombe and the Belgians have everything planned out to protect their interests.'

'And ours too, let's not forget,' Dillon added, leaning forward in agreement, taking a long gulp from his glass.

'Yes, and ours too,' Penderel reiterated. The pen fiddling had ceased. 'We are generally aligned, though the Belgians don't pretend to favor independence. The U.S. needs to publicly support a democratic election. If Lumumba is elected Prime Minister – which we expect -- and he does not share our national interests, then we have a problem.'

Penderel watched Dillon for a reaction. His face was alert, listening, but non-committal. 'The U.N. and the Belgians have their interests, too. And they are not remotely compatible.'

Dillon nodded as he took a last gulp. 'We should let those parties take the lead, then,' he answered, sitting back in the chair, appearing content with what he heard. 'Nothing gained by publicly sticking our nose under that tent. That's a circus tent, full of snake charmers and acrobats. Let's see what happens.'

'We have identified supportive coalitions of the most promising leaders,' Penderel continued, trying to finish his asessment. He felt calm now. 'We know who is pro-U.S.

and are trying to help them forge a coalition. Not something they're used to. It's a land of petty kings and tribes.'

'Boy, do I know that! This *whole* continent is about petty tribesmen. But the big issues are the same. At least we're dealing with Christians. Getting between the French and the bedouins in Algeria has been a thankless job.' Dillon was satisfied, the best Penderel could tell. He had polished off his scotch in three swallows and was now chewing on the purified ice cubes.

'Remember we have our own elections coming up in five months,' he continued, thumping the glass on the table sharply. 'Our tribes have different perspectives too. We need to be prepared for a shift in priorities.'

'That makes sense.'

'Well, sorry to drink and run,' said Dillon. 'Flight leaves in a little over an hour. It was nice to finally meet you. Your assessment is sound. Keep listening hard.' Dillon rose, gave Penderel a firm handshake and turned to walk out of the bar.

'Have a safe trip, sir,' Penderel waved. 'It was a pleasure to meet you.'

Penderel left the Grand Hotel. He didn't envy Dillon's job, ping ponging around a hot, uncomfortable continent in the midst of change. The next three months would be hell on him – eleven new and unproven countries would be gaining independence.

There was so much opportunity for error or mischief.

Penderel and Dillon had spent twenty minutes together. For Penderel, it was a chance to see brilliance in motion and to show off his intelligence skills. To Dillon, it was his third meeting of the day and he was on his way to the Norfolk Hotel at 2200 to debrief another agent worried about what to do with Kenyatta and the pain-in-the-ass Brits.

Penderel got into a cab and headed over to UMHK to meet Biver. He thought about the meeting with Dillon. He was pleased that he didn't screw up. Dillon had said *your assessment is sound.* That was high praise from a man not known for compliments. Penderel felt like he was finally getting the hang of the job, though its rhythms and the constant overhang of an unaccomplished mission still took getting used to. Clandestine work never seemed to be fully accomplished.

Penderel doubted that Dillon would relay his praise to Denman, though he hoped it might come up in passing. He had to remind himself that people in this business didn't get medals and pats on the back. And there was no success yet. Everything was riding on this election and it was impossible to predict how it would unfold.

Next up was Jean-Pierre Biver. He had asked Penderel to drop by the office to discuss something that he was not able to completely convey over lunch. He needed reassurance that the rumors about Lumumba planning to nationalize the mining industry were just that.

But Penderel didn't blame Biver for being nervous. He couldn't afford to to take any chances. Everyone knew that this was the only place in the whole country that would operate normally after June 30th.

Thirteen

Late June 1960

June 29th arrived. The thick air of Léopoldville was steamy. The U.S. consulate staff watched and prayed for a smooth three-day celebration. The King of Belgium was due to land at the airport within the next half-hour and events had been planned to mark the formal handover of power.

The last month had been trying, with much back room wrangling, agreements to coalitions, backtracking, money movement and proclamations. Lumumba's MNC-L party won the national election with one-quarter of the seats, but it had taken three weeks to form a governing coalition.

Penderel knew that this was likely. Justin-Marie Bomboko had pointed out that the Constitutional Convention in Philadelphia was far more contentious, with a less effective outcome. They all had to be patient, let this country learn and make mistakes. Still, Penderel believed the Belgians had been too hands-off, too disengaged, like a pouty child, unhappy with being spurned and ready to walk away. He, Tucci and Denman had tried to get Delvaux to play a more constructive role with his diplomatic corps, but they were consumed with getting their citizens safely out.

The nervousness the prior month had mutated into cynical detachment – except of course in Katanga. Penderel was concerned about the lack of anxiousness in Elisabethville the last few weeks since his visit. It had been calm, quiet and businesslike. Tshombe had asked more questions about where he was to sit on the podium in the ceremony than what a centralized form of government meant to his province. It was too quiet for Penderel's comfort.

The agreement hammered out by the Chamber and the Senate named Lumumba as Prime Minister and Joseph Kasavubu as President. Penderel was happy that Kasavubu would be president. He was uninspiring, but he led a moderate group to counterbalance Lumumba's populism. Bomboko was right -- Kasavubu wasn't a revolutionary. He and Lumumba were rivals who detested one another, but they both understood the stakes for working together to create a unified Congo.

There had been small skirmishes, but most of the country's energy poured into the visible ceremony of independence. Despite their ineptitude in all other areas, the Belgians were very good at teaching their students about parades, sharp-looking uniforms and brass bands.

King Baudouin's motorcade advanced from the airport into town along the soon-to-be-renamed Boulevard du 30 Juin. It was a joyous, clear day, marked by bright skies, military marching bands and schoolchildren in uniforms. There were lines of wellwishers, standing four-deep along the parade route, cheering and waving the new blue, red and gold flags of the Republic of Congo.

Denman, Penderel and Tucci watched the grainy black and white footage over the television in the consulate. 'So far, so good,' noted Tucci. 'It looks pretty orderly. Kasavubu is riding alongside of the King in the open convertible. It's quite a show. Did you know they don't even have a national anthem yet? They're going to play 'Marching Through Georgia.'

'Hey Penderel, did you hear that?' Denman asked, laughing. 'You're a Southerner, right? Isn't that about Sherman burning down Atlanta?'

'I believe so. They play it everywhere,' he answered flatly. 'Hell, the Brits sang it parading through India!' He smiled and turned to his boss. 'Does Belgium have a national anthem? They barely have a nation.'

'If they do,' said Tucci tartly. 'It's probably a be-bop piano and harmonica version of 'La Marseillaise' and 'Het Wilhelmus' pushed together and performed by Toots Thielmans.

'Aren't you the music man?' remarked Penderel. 'How about a little champagne?'

Penderel walked to the refrigerator and returned with a chilled bottle and six glasses. Timberlake was at the ambassador's residence with his wife Julie getting dressed and writing a short set of remarks for a reception for the King in two hours. Today was a day of celebration, even for the Americans at the consulate.

Both Denman and Tucci cheered, as did Jerry the radio operator and Sarah, the special attaché who handled a lot of the encoding and correspondence. 'To success for the new Republic of Congo,' they shouted, raising their flutes.

'They really need a new name,' Tucci commented laughing. 'There's going to be another Republic of Congo across the river next month. If this place goes to hell, we can just say we worked in the other Congo.'

'Appears Lumumba is behaving himself so far' said Penderel, sipping the champagne. 'Look at the natty bow tie and suit he has on! What a hepcat? Maybe he could be in the band?' Lumumba walked jauntily beside the motorcade, waving like an entertainer.

'Look at this!' Denman screamed, pointing at the TV set. 'Some guy just stole the King's sword! I'm not kidding. *Look!* He's dancing around like a high-stepping drum major. *Oh my God!*'

The images on the screen of a well-dressed man in a

suit and tie triumphantly raising and lowering the ceremonial sword that he grabbed out of the backseat of the limousine were comical, if not foreshadowing. Particularly as the King and Kasavubu didn't notice at first and kept waving to the crowd.

The security detail immediately arrested the man and the parade continued toward the Parliament building. Denman looked over at Penderel and began to laugh uncontrollably. Tucci poured the last of the champagne and shook his head. 'Unbelievable. *Un-fucking-believable*!'

Tucci, Penderel and Denman arrived early the next morning at the Parliament building and were ushered to their seats in the upstairs gallery. Sixty-five countries sent representatives to the ceremony. The independence of Congo had become a worldwide obsession in the press. The morning schedule called for a speech by the King. Independence would be granted at midnight. The King took to the podium and began:

'The independence of the Congo is the crowning of the work conceived by the genius of King Leopold II undertaken by him with firm courage, and continued by Belgium with perseverance.'

Denman turned sideways, eyes larger than dinner plates and stared at Penderel and Tucci. He was speechless at the reference to 'King Leopold II' and 'courage' in the same sentence. His mouth was frozen wide open in pantomine.

'For eighty years, Belgium has sent your land the best of her sons, first to deliver the Congo basin from the odious slave trade which was decimating its population. Later to bring together the different tribes which are now preparing to form the greatest independent state of Africa. It is your job, gentlemen, to show that we were right in trusting you.'

Tucci's jaw dropped as he turned to Denman and Penderel. 'Are you getting a load of this? Does this clown have a clue what he's saying?'

'Something about 'showing us that *we were right in trusting you*?' Denman answered.

'Yep, and the praise toward his great uncle, Leo II,' Tucci answered, steamed at the patronizing tone of the speech. 'He's the motherfucker who started this whole fucking mess! The same guy who started the Congo Free State as his private bank. The prick that enslaved this country and picked it clean of ivory and rubber! Did he really say, 'Deliver the Congo basin from the *odious slave trade*?' Un-fucking-believable! I can't believe he is saying this. Oh-my-God.'

There was a slow, rolling but audible roar through the crowd as the King spoke. The new leadership of the country that included Victor Nendaka, the new head of the *Sûreté Nationale du Congo*, Moise Tshombe, President of the Province of Katanga and Joseph-Marie Bomboko, the minister of Foreign Affairs sat on the stage, stunned and shaken as the King droned on.

Lumumba was sitting on the podium, visibly agitated, corkscrewing his neck like a bird that had eaten a frog. He wasn't scheduled to speak. The Belgians and the new Congolese leadership agreed this day was about celebration and coming together. It was not about expressing disappointment or division.

Lumumba rose slowly, sharp eyes glaring ahead, expressionless. There was a gasp in the audience. He had no script to read from, but he was going to speak anyway.

Tucci looked up. 'Oh boy, this is going from bad to worse. Hold on, gents.'

Lumumba walked deliberately toward the podium. The large hall was completely silent. The only sound was the loud clicking of his newly soled and shined shoes. Denman leaned forward in his chair, looking down at the stage. Penderel sat back gingerly. Tucci held his breath, before noisily exhaling. Lumumba glared at the audience.

His body posture was coiled, but his movement was measured and controlled. His voice -- the voice of a country's anger, confusion and repression – started quietly, but immediately became emotional. His was the voice of a people finally on their own to a place beyond their imaginations. A place not remotely prepared to be independent without guidance.

'Men and women of the Congo, victorious independence fighters, I salute you in the name of the Congolese Government.' He gathered himself as he looked out to the silent audience. He paused

and smiled, as a roar went up from the back of the great hall.

'Although this independence of the Congo is being proclaimed today by agreement, no Congolese will ever forget that independence was won in struggle, a struggle, in which we were undaunted by privation or suffering and stinted neither strength nor blood.'

An intense sternness came to his taut face at the point on his chin where a tightly cropped, devilish beard ended.

'It was filled with tears, fire and blood. We are deeply proud of our struggle to put an end to the humiliating bondage forced upon us. That was our lot for the eighty years of colonial rule. Our wounds are too fresh and much too painful to be forgotten.'

Cheers roared up from the streets outside, where makeshift antennas were strewn atop corrugated shacks. Large tin megaphones were placed on tables and flipped trashcans, so that ordinary Congolese could hear the ceremony. They had not expected this. The King and the Belgians in attendance were flabbergasted. The Americans sitting in the balcony were nearly speechless.

'I hope to hell they are serving martinis at this luncheon. I expect everyone will be blotto by tonight,' Penderel snickered as they filed out of the balcony in the Parliament building. He spotted Rene Delvaux walking out with the Belgian delegation. He looked up to see Penderel and waved him off. There would be time later to put this all in perspective and share a proper ten-ounce Black Label.

'Goddammit,' yelled Denman, turning to Tucci and Penderel. 'We all knew this would happen. The fucking Belgians would fuck this up. They promised they would manage this. Look at the mess they have created here.' Penderel paused and looked down at the floor of the Parliament Building. There were still pediments and columns supporting the enormous structure that still needed another coat of white paint. The row of chairs on the podium smartly hid sections of ungrouted marble behind the stage.

A loud roar of muffled, but angry voices rose and echoed in the space. Instead of a consonant group exiting in pride and unison, small groups, white and black gestured and hatched plans among themselves, oblivious to their fellow citizens. No one was ready for this moment.

Fourteen

Early July to Mid August 1960

'Don't tell me,' Timberlake stared across the table. 'This has been the longest week of my life and we're only on day four.'

Denman looked up, shaking his head. 'Sorry, Tim. This is going to wreak havoc. We just heard that Lumumba called for a pay raise for all government employees. *Except* for the white officers of the *Force Publique*. That caused that idiot General Janssens to refuse to 'Africanize' the officer corps.'

'What do you mean refuse to 'Africanize' the officer corps?' Timberlake answered. 'That was always part of the plan. This is an African country! Goddammit! What in the hell is going on?'

On July 6th, Congolese soldiers mutinied against the white officers and attacked Europeans. A day later, armed bands roamed the capital and larger cities, looting and terrorizing the white population. Within a week of independence, a civil war had taken shape.

Penderel was returning from the port where he had put Habib Khouri's wife and two children on a ferry over to Brazzaville. Khouri stayed – at least for now, although Penderel had urged him to go, at least until things settled down. The consulate's driver Antoine was anxious as they drove into the city center towards the embassy.

In just a few days' time, the city had become lawless. Drunk, angry, unsupervised soldiers prowled the streets, firing their weapons into the sky, menacing the white citizenry. It was the haunting premonition Penderel had back in January.

Penderel watched from the back seat of the car as three soldiers looted a small shop in the center of town in the middle of the day. Some gangs of soldiers were on the move, others sat along median strips under the trees, drinking beer and smoking marijuana.

'Just keep moving, Antoine,' Penderel said, trying to calm his driver. 'We have diplomatic plates. They won't bother us.'

'They don't care sir,' he answered, looking back in the mirror. 'They think all westerners are Belgians.'

'I can't believe this happened so quickly. We expected problems, but not this. This city is a war zone. I suspect the Belgian army will be here shortly.'

'Can they do that?' Antoine asked. 'Aren't we a sovereign nation now?'

'Yes, but ...' Penderel began. Then he stopped speaking. Three soldiers had surrounded the small car and opened the passenger and rear doors. A few moments earlier, they were laughing and sitting in the dirt in the median strip. One jumped into the front, while the other two sandwiched Penderel in the back seat. Penderel could smell stale beer and marijuana on their breaths. Their uniforms were soiled and soaked. 'You,' the one in the front said to Antoine, 'Drive ahead.'

'Wait,' Penderel said. 'I am an American diplomat.' He pulled out his passport, but the man in the front dismissed the gesture with a wave of his hand.

'Insensé,' he shrugged.

The tidy European residential part of the city disappeared into the rear view mirror as the stressed-out 1957 white Renault Dauphine puttered toward the ring of slums. Penderel could see an already steamy city, smoldering. Bands of soldiers had overturned trashcans and set them ablaze. Other gangs not in uniform were looting small shops and tossing chunks of masonry from the construction sites of unfinished buildings through windows.

There were no sirens or men in spit-shined uniforms, like he witnessed the first day. The soldier in the front seat yelled at Antoine to pull over ahead at a dilapidated industrial building on a trash-strewn, unpaved road.

'Sortez par ici le long de la rue,' the one in the front seat barked. Penderel sat motionless, breathing hard. *I'm not getting out.*

'Sortez de la voiture,' he screamed again, pointing his ancient Browning HP revolver at Antoine. *Get out of the car!*

The group hurriedly entered a hot, stuffy, dimly lit room. Several soldiers were sitting in a circle on the concrete floor, smoking dope and passing a bottle of cognac around. They were speaking in Lingala.

'What are they saying, Antoine?'

'Something about you having to kiss his foot.'

A tall scarecrow wearing a tattered beret walked toward Penderel, with his boot in hand. The others giggled and nudged each other. 'Come over here and kiss my foot, *flamand*.'

'I told you I'm an American diplomat. I'm not Flemish. And no, I will not kiss your foot.'

'If I say you will, you will,' he answered. He sat down on a small chair that looked to be made for an elementary school classroom. His bent long limbs made him look like a praying mantis.

'I'm an American diplomat. I demand you release me and my assistant immediately.'

The tall soldier stood and smiled to his colleagues. Some were paying attention; two others had wandered into another room, leading Antoine away. 'Ever played Russian roulette?' He took his revolver from the holster, turned towards the circle of soldiers, appearing to remove bullets from the chamber.

Penderel shook his head, as the others looked on disinterestedly, passing the remainder of the Hennessey around. The room was steamy and smelled of urine, rotting garbage and filth.

'No? Then I will do it for you.' He turned from the group and put the gun to Penderel's head.

'*Merde*,' Penderel screamed, as the soldier pulled the trigger. The pistol's hammer clicked as it hit an empty chamber.

'Now kiss my foot,' he said grinning, pointing the gun again at Penderel. Then he fired the gun again. Another click. 'Ha ha ha,' he screeched.

'Do you know that the Geneva Convention has rules for how prisoners are treated? You kill me and that will be it for you. You can't just capture and threaten diplomats!'

'Just kiss my foot, patron, and you have nothing to fear,' he said. 'Two chances wasted.'

Penderel again shook his head.

The soldier pointed the gun again at Penderel's temple and pulled the trigger three times. *Click, click, click.*

'Last chance, patron,' he said laughing now. 'Kiss this foot.'

'To hell with you, release me now,' Penderel yelled as the soldier fired the empty chamber one last time. Then he and the others started laughing at Penderel, as he put the revolver back in the holster. One of the others stood up from the circle and offered Penderel some wine that they had just opened. The cognac bottle was empty and in several pieces in the corner of the room.

'Americans are good. We love America!' he yelled, giving Penderel a hug. The tall man was bony and smelled like a sewer. Penderel wanted to squeeze him to death.

Penderel shook his head as they all howled. 'Here's to USA, USA,' they chanted, passing the wine bottle around. '*USA, USA, USA*.' Penderel took a sip and shook his head. *What a fucking day?*

'Yes, the USA is here to help you,' said Penderel in broken French, still shaken and breathless. *Oui, les États-Unis sont là pour vous aider*. Despite the celebratory toasting, he was unconvinced that they were safe yet. But the stringy leader had lost his energy as he sat back in the tiny chair, motioning for the bottle of wine.

'Vous êtes libre partir,' he yelled towards them with his

arm. 'Dégagez-vous, pauvre type!' he cackled as his weary, drunk friends laughed and waved dismissal.

Antoine and Penderel drove back into town silently, with the car windows up and doors locked. They were stunned that the city had become that dangerous, that soon after independence. Finally, Antoine turned and asked, 'Are you all right, Monsieur?'

'Yes,' he said, lying. Despite all of his exposure to war and violence, this was the first time Penderel had ever been held up at gunpoint. Yet his principal occupation up to joining the CIA was to use a gun to kill people. He'd never thought of it that way, until that moment. He defined himself as a soldier; others called him a war hero. But this incident had scared Richard Penderel and he was shaken. Now he wasn't sure what he was.

'When are the Belgians coming?'

'I'm guessing soon,' Penderel answered. 'But not soon enough.' *What a fucking day!* His ears were ringing and he felt faint, exhausted from the ordeal and the sudden descent in chaos.

The U.S. Embassy population had swelled to nearly thirty, as scared Americans and Europeans sought refuge. There was no civil order in Léopoldville and Stanleyville. Only Elisabethville appeared to be in control, though there were scattered riots there too. He suspected contingency plans were well underway.

'Don't tell me,' Ambassador Timberlake sighed, as an urgent cable came through on the morning of July 11th. Six thousand Belgian troops had landed in Elisabethville and Moise Tshombe had announced the independence of the State of Katanga. He simply said the province was 'seceding from chaos.'

'This has been in the wind for months,' said Denman nonchalantly, re-reading the cable. 'We all knew that. Belgium was simply not going to allow their interests and ours – I might add – to fall into the wrong hands. This is good news. You want all of that cobalt under control of that joke of an army? God help us all.'

'Maybe so,' said Tucci. 'But we cannot publicly approve of a foreign country invading a country that's not even two weeks old. Lumumba will bitch to the U.N. and demand the troops be withdrawn. Dicky, can you call Biver?'

'Yep,' he answered. 'I've tried him nearly every day and he's not returned my calls. I'll try again, but I suspect I won't get anywhere.'

'Stay on it,' Timberlake said. 'Katanga is one thing. I worry about other regions like South Kivu doing the same. They're sitting on all the diamonds. Boy, what a fucking mess!'

'Meanwhile, we need to get some protection here,'

Timberlake said. 'This place was never designed to be a fortress.' He was right. The lobby of the embassy had glass doors and the brick latticework decorating the side of the building were a ready-made ladder for anyone who wanted to climb through the windows of the second or third floors.

The promised contingent of U.S. Marines had yet to arrive. The only weapons that the embassy had were six tear gas grenades. 'Dicky, can you shake some trees out there?'

'Yes, sir.' Penderel called the Belgian Embassy. He had his own crisis to manage, but Delvaux took Penderel's call. 'What in the hell is going on?'

'We're trying to save our citizens. No one expected this.'

'I'm not calling to scold you,' Penderel replied slowly. 'We need some weapons to protect ourselves. Anything you have or can point us to?'

'We have two old Browning semi-automatic pistols and a box of Czech fragmentation grenades that were left at the airport. They're yours, if you can get here.'

'Thanks,' said Penderel, hanging up. 'Antoine, we have a mission,' he called out as they left the relative safety of the consulate to go arms shopping.

On July 17th, the President and the Prime Minister addressed an ultimatum to the Secretary-General of the United Nations, warning that if the Belgian forces were not completely withdrawn within 48 hours, they would request troops from the Soviet Union. The resolution and threat of Soviet action spooked everyone.

Belgian troops withdrew within a week, except of course, from Katanga. The immediate crisis was resolved, though the perceived competence of the new government was in freefall.

In his first seventeen days in office, the new, charismatic Prime Minister faced an army uprising for which he was partly responsible, the secession of the country's wealthiest province, while presiding over a government paralyzed by personal and tribal rivalries. The army mutiny also produced a mass flight of Belgian businessman, technicians, senior military and police officers that effectively brought his nascent independent country's economy to a halt.

The U.S. embassy team realized that Lumumba was unqualified and his threat to turn to the Soviet Union for help was unacceptable. In mid-August, Lumumba followed through and requested Soviet assistance to tamp down the insurrection in Katanga. That was all the justification that the Eisenhower administration needed.

'Get your ass back to Katanga,' said Denman to Penderel. 'New plans are afoot.'

Elisabethville had the look of an orderly war zone. Belgian troops and the Katangan gendarmerie were visible along the highway coming in from the airport, but traffic and the rhythms of the city looked normal. Word had it that members of the *Force Publique* evaporated back into the population, rather than face down the well armed, disciplined forces of the separatist state. It didn't appear as though the Red Army was invading the capital city.

Those who resisted had been chased into the northeast or slaughtered. Penderel had to give Biver and Tshombe credit – they did what they said they'd do and really never telegraphed otherwise. Katanga would continue to operate as it had for the past fifty years.

Denman had given Penderel instructions to tell Tshombe that the U.S. would support any effort to prevent the Soviets from getting a foothold in the north, but could not directly be involved in Lumumba's removal. That provided a lot of leeway for interpretation. He had planned meetings first with Biver, then Tshombe and if he was lucky, a nice meal with Beryl Reader. They had not connected since before the election and its bloody aftermath.

Everyone's prophecy had come true – the country had split up, Lumumba was ineffectual and the Soviets had infiltrated the weak government. The only thing different on this trip was a small contingent of white military guards surrounding the UMHK headquarters on Avenue de l'Etouile across from the zoo.

'So, Mr. Penderel,' Biver began. 'Did you know Mr. Lumumba made the request to the Soviet Union for support? Hardly a surprise, do you think?'

'It obviously concerns us. And frankly we are surprised this occurred now. I don't think he expected that things would unravel so quickly.'

'He's not fit to govern. You *do* recognize that? You were well aware that this was the likely outcome, weren't you?'

'Yes, Jean-Pierre, we did.' Penderel didn't like Biver's patronizing tone. It was not like him to be that critical. The events over the past few weeks had even unnerved the most powerful man in the country.

'Is the United States prepared to assist in his removal?'

'We are prepared to help the country transition to more effective leadership, provided it is done according to the constitution. There are several ways that we are studying. To you my friend, is the State of Katanga willing to rejoin the country, if we can help create a stable central government?'

'That is a question I cannot answer,' said Biver.

'Well, I think we need some assurances that take everyone's interests into account.'

'I thought the United States was a loyal and trustworthy ally of this company and what this province provides?'

'We are, but we also need to stand for what is right in the eyes of the world,' said Penderel. 'Unlike Belgium, we have a global leadership role that requires taking competing interests into account. All we need is Khrushchev whining to the U.N. about us taking sides and we lose the whole continent of Africa.'

'You will need to speak to President Tshombe.'

'Jean-Pierre, I've been sent to assure you that we will support any and all efforts to prevent this country and this province from Soviet infiltration. Is this clear?'

'Yes, it is, Mr. Penderel. You may want to speak with Mr. Reader and Count d'Aspremont on your visit. They have some different perspectives.'

'No doubt,' said Penderel. The scuttlebutt around Léopoldville was the Belgians were planning to take Lumumba out. Habib Khouri had hinted at it, though he remarked that the Belgians talking about it were inebriated and blowing off steam. 'But certainly that needs to be carefully considered. I will call them.'

'I understand and am glad you have come to visit. Perhaps an early dinner? Say 6:30?' Biver suggested, changing tone. The Belgians were funny, often prickly people, but they always left room for the rituals of entertainment.

'Of course.'

Moise Tshombe sat in an enormous mahogany chair at the end of a large room at the rear of the palace. The desk was equally large and he had a few papers on it that didn't appear to have been touched. Penderel could hear the echo of his heels crossing the expanse of the office.

To Penderel, it appeared he was really a king – with all the trappings of power, without the anxieties of day-to-day governance. Two bodyguards stood at the entrance to his office, but otherwise it was empty. As always, Tshombe stood and graciously boomed out a warm welcome and handshake to Penderel.

'I expect you're here to discuss our withdrawal from the mayhem?' Tshombe asked. He'd prepared for Penderel's visit.

'Yes, I guess that's one way of putting it.'

'And you know, we have problems in the north with rebels trying to destabilize the state. And they have guns, too. AK-47s. Guns are too much for these stupid chaps,' he laughed. 'They're used to panga knives.'

'President Tshombe, I'm here on behalf of the U.S. government to request that you rejoin the Republic. Without Katanga, this country is doomed to stay divided and fail.' Penderel looked at him intently.

'Richard, we've had this discussion several times before,' Tshombe began firmly, yet calmly. 'Until there is a functioning body capable of holding this federation together – and I do mean *a federation* – then there is no sense talking.'

'You know that risks U.N. involvement, sir? That's not good for anyone.'

'Yes, I do,' Tshombe replied. 'But I'm really not concerned with them. They will huff and puff and threaten to blow my house down, but as you can see,' he said with open palms, 'this is a very sturdy house. The thing that most concerns me – and it should you too – is the Soviet Union. Do you really want another Cuba looking after the world's most productive uranium mines?'

This was always the issue that Penderel and the U.S. had no answer to and everyone knew it. The conversation always went this way and always would.

Penderel chuckled. 'No, President Tshombe, you know the answer to that.'

'My advice to you,' Tshombe said gently, but forcefully,

'is to get Mr. Lumumba to start acting like a leader. I've known Patrice for a decade and admire his zeal and patriotism. But he needs to run this country with intelligence and balance. Lest he will be deposed.'

Penderel knew that this conversation was over.

Timothy Reader stood before the firing range. It was early afternoon and he hoped to get back to Elisabethville by dark. At this rate, it would be a few weeks before he could trust these young knuckleheads with guns. Count d'Aspremont wanted new recruits to get some training with weapons, before sending them into North Katanga and Stanleyville.

They were a mismatched collection of moon-faced farm boys, eager to get into it, but too stupid to get out of it. The Rhodesians and South Africans whom Reader knew were more self-sufficient than this sorry lot. There were twenty Kenyans, a half-dozen from the Ugandan Protectorate and probably ten South Africans from Durban.

'Is this a babysitting service, Mike?' Reader asked, shaking his head. Mike Hoare, an Irishman relocated to Durban was also involved in attempting to transform this caboodle of boys into a combat-ready corps. 'These fellows are not fit. Look at that one,' said Reader, pointing to a chubby-faced boy who trailed the group running the obstacle course by several hundred yards. 'He weighs more than I do.'

'I told you it would take time,' Hoare responded. 'Give 'em two months and they'll be fine. Just remember whom they'll be fighting against. At least our boys will have rifles.'

'So do the bloody kaffirs. That's the goddamned problem!'

'Hey, Timmy, call for you. I think it's the wife.' Bob Denard, a French soldier and veteran of the Indochina and Algerian wars, yelled, poking his head out of the office.

Reader strode over to the farmhouse and picked up the phone. 'Yeah,' he answered.

'No I don't think I can get back in by dinner. Probably home late.' Reader paused and nodded. 'Tell everyone hello. Sorry I can't make it.' He hung up the phone and returned to the firing range.

'Missing a nice dinner in town with the American guy and Biver for these wankers,' Reader lamented to Hoare, who was screaming at the new recruits as they scaled the eight-foot wall adjacent to the firing range. 'We could use that Yank out here. The SOB can shoot a gun.'

'I've heard of him – Penderel right?' Hoare answered. 'The CIA's got him as an agent now? Is he any good?'

'Hard to tell,' said Reader. 'Had him down to the farm a few months back. Seems like a nice enough chap … for a bloody Yank. Sense my wife's taken a fancy to him.'

'Oh, Timmy,' answered Hoare. 'You know how she is when she gets on the piss. Women like to flirt, that's all. I'd pay it no mind.'

'I don't, mate, but it makes me mad as hell. She gets all jittery when someone new shows up. Then she gets into the champagne and makes an ass of herself. I'll kill the both of them if anything happens.'

'Save it for the Balubas and our Prime Minister.'

'I'm sorry Timothy couldn't be here tonight,' Beryl commented as they sat down to dinner at 7 p.m. It was an informal dinner at the Bivers' city residence on Avenue du Tanganika. Downtown Elisabethville was very compact and the city prided itself on its walkability and low crime rate. 'He's up in the north doing God knows what.'

Biver looked up and smiled. 'Oh, he's helping us with some logistical security matters. Thought he'd be back by now.'

'Security?' Beryl asked. 'Hmmm.'

'Yes, we have some challenges with the current crisis and our railroads,' he answered quickly.

'Since the election, everything has changed,' lamented Libellule. 'Everyone must be more cautious now.'

'Well, it's far better here than in other parts of the

country,' said Penderel. 'Separation has its advantages.'

Everyone giggled nervously before Beryl rescued the awkward silence. 'Oh, we're all friends now. Let's not talk about politics again! It's over and done with, let's move on.' She paused, lighting a cigarette. 'Please tell me your thoughts on the divine-looking John F. Kennedy. What a dreamboat! Will he be your next President?'

'I thought we were avoiding politics?' said Biver, 'but this is, at least, new ground. He's a war hero too. Right?'

'So I hear,' said Penderel. 'He's got a good publicist that's for sure. Richer than Croesus. His dad made a lot of money bootlegging whiskey during the Prohibition. He's Catholic too.'

'What does that mean?' said Libellule surprised. 'Is that bad? I'm Catholic. So is Jean-Pierre.' She seemed alarmed that being Catholic was an issue in an American election.

'It's probably not a big issue,' Penderel answered. 'America is conservative in many ways. But the country is changing. Young people are becoming rebellious. This new rock 'n roll music has all the older people worried. At least they were when I left.'

'I heard that one of the rockers, Jerry Lewis, married his thirteen-year-old cousin,' Beryl laughed. 'He'd probably fit right in in Rhodesia.'

'I thought Jerry Lewis was a comedian?' said Biver. 'He had that act with Dean Martin, didn't he?'

'It's confusing,' laughed Penderel. 'Jerry *Lee* Lewis is the musician who married his cousin, 'Whole Lotta' Shakin' going on. Remember that song? Jerry Lewis is a comedian. The French really like him for some reason.'

'No accounting for the French taste,' Libellule said snobbishly. Both Biver and Penderel glanced across the table, silently raising their glasses.

'It's getting late,' Beryl said, looking at her watch. It was 8:30 and the Bivers' staff had promptly cleared the dessert plates and coffee cups.

'Richard, do you mind seeing that Beryl gets home safely?' asked Biver. 'The streets are safe, but one can never take too many precautions.'

'Of course,' he said. 'It's my pleasure.'

'It's only a few blocks,' Beryl answered. 'I'll be fine. Timothy should be home in a little while.'

'Don't be silly, Beryl. I'll see you home. Thank you both for a lovely dinner,' said Penderel, getting up. 'It's nice to have a home-cooked meal.'

Penderel felt coolness in the air as he escorted Beryl back to her townhouse. He had not brought an outercoat, so it was nice that Beryl strolled inside his stride with her large oatmeal colored cashmire scarf. Her Vol de Nuit lingered in the air as they walked along Avenue du Kasai.

This was the moment Penderel had waited for, but tonight she was sober and quieter than usual.

'That was a lovely evening. Very low key. Thank you for being my protector,' she said stopping in front of a grand house off the Plaza Royale. 'I'd invite you in, but my husband is returning tonight.'

Penderel moved closer and put his arms around Beryl. He looked down to give her a goodnight kiss and she stuck her tongue forcefully into his mouth.

Her ferocity and strength took Penderel back, but he engaged equally. They were like two wrestlers, grabbing each other's hair and awkwardly trying to touch one another without falling over. Penderel caressed her bosoms and he could feel an erect nipple through her brassiere.

Beryl in turn stroked his penis through his pants and smiled, as it got harder. Penderel slid his right hand into her wet crotch and watched her eyes widen, then close. Suddenly, she caught her breath and pulled away.

'I'm sorry, I can't do this.' Her hair was mussed-up and her pulse thumped through her chest. Her voice quivered like that time in the Memling restaurant three months earlier. The intensity in her eyes suggested that she wanted nothing more than to have sex right there on the sidewalk.

'We could go inside,' Penderel urged, leading her up the steps. 'Let's go!'

Beryl looked around, left, then right. She was still

panting hard, trying to catch her breath. The street was dead quiet, without a soul on it. She paused. But she knew this city had eyes everywhere and she was probably already in trouble. 'I can't, I really can't.' She fiddled for her keys in her clutch, but her hands were shaking. 'You'd better go. It's best for both of us. Really it is. Trust me.'

'I understand,' said Penderel, watching her climb the steps, unlock the door agitatedly and shut it behind her.

Fifteen

Late August to Mid September 1960

'We conclude that his removal must be an urgent and prime objective and that under existing conditions this should be a high priority of our covert action.'

Denman stared at the cable, signed by Allen Dulles, the director for Central Intelligence. It was another steamy day, though Léopoldville had quieted down as the army had begun to operate more effectively. Thank heaven Joseph Mobutu had gotten control of the army! At least they could leave the embassy and resume discussions with contacts, now more important than ever to U.S. goals in the country. It was too bad that Lumumba continued to be so irrational and unsteady. But at least one facet of the country was working.

Denman liked Mobutu. He was one of the few people who had focus. Though he was comically skinny, had large ears and wore large Buddy Holly glasses, he had a remarkable presence and force of personality that he ably displayed in bringing order to the army. He was the complete opposite of Lumumba: thoughtful, measured and pragmatic. He was known to regularly work eighteen-hour days and never forgot a name.

Denman had slowly built his relationship with Mobutu and even hoped to bring him under the Langley tent. The cascade of events over the past month and Dulles' unambiguous cable accelerated that plan.

'The Soviets are pouring into the country. You must know that, Mr. Denman?' Mobutu asked. It was late and Denman had come to discuss the CIA's concerns with the Chief of the Army.

He nodded. Denman had hired a man at the airport to count any white men getting off Soviet aircraft. In a six-week period, approximately 1,000 'conseillers techniques' arrived at N'djili.

'I know we don't have enough educated Congolese to fill the shoes of the Belgian civil servants who have left the country. But that doesn't mean I want Soviet technicians to take their places. We didn't fight for independence to have another country re-colonize us!'

Denman stared at the persuasive young army colonel as he returned with some books and pamphlets that had been handed out to his troops. It looked to be Marxist propaganda, printed in English. One pamphlet title said, 'The Revolution Is Now' with three dashing Slavic models saluting a stylized sketch of Stalin and Lenin. Another had a cartoon of a bearded Arab fighter in a *dishdasha* holding a rifle.

'Look at this stuff!' Mobutu laughed. 'Complete shit! Lucky no one in the Army can read English. Except for me!'

'Lumumba swore that he would keep the Soviets away from the army. He hasn't kept his word. Not to me, nor to my army! So … what it comes down to is this: I've called all of my area commanders to Léopoldville to discuss the Soviet problem. They are all as unhappy about Soviet efforts to penetrate the army as I am.'

Denman remained silent, but could see where this was heading. Mobutu stood up from his chair and walked to the window, turning. 'I've called all of my area commanders to Léopoldville to discuss the Soviet problem. They are as unhappy about Soviet efforts to penetrate the army as I am.

'The army is prepared to overthrow Lumumba,' Mobutu continued. 'But only on the condition that the United States recognize the government that would replace Lumumba's. The government we establish will be temporary. I will stay in power only long enough to get the Soviets out of the Congo and to create a democratic regime.'

Denman sat back, absorbing what he had just heard. Dulles wanted Lumumba out, but he assumed that meant through some form of legal or parliamentary change, not an army coup.

'I've got to get back to my commanders,' he said flatly. 'I have to give them a 'go' or a 'no go' order tonight.'

Denman looked up. Mobutu's intensity was burning a hole in his chest. 'Mr. Mobutu, I can assure you the United States government will recognize a temporary government composed of civilian technocrats.'

'The army takeover will take place within the next three weeks,' he said. 'I will need $5,000 to provide for my senior officers. If this action fails, we will all be in prison or dead. The money will be for our families.

'My area commanders are all noncommissioned officers and poorly paid so their families will not expect a large sum. But I have to assure them that they will not be destitute.'

'The money will be available in the morning. Or rather later this morning,' Denman said, looking at his watch. It was nearly 2 a.m.

Denman left Mobutu's office in a hurry, mind racing, concerned he had overstepped his authority. *Got to get to Timberlake. Then cable Langley.* The streets were quiet and a moist haze hung over the streetlights, like Spanish moss. This was not the provincial backwater post he'd expected.

'It must be important if you are here at this hour,' Ambassador Timberlake groggily mumbled, answering the doorbell at the residence. 'Let me put a robe on and I'll be right down. Fix yourself a drink and while you're at it, make one for me. A neat Scotch.'

Denman relayed the story, detail by detail, as Timberlake listened, sipping his drink. 'George, tell me something. Do you have a personal fortune or enough service time to qualify for retirement?'

Denman smiled, shaking his head.

'Well, as it happens, I have both. If the coup fails, the two of us will be out of a job.'

'Do you think I should contact Mobutu and withdraw my guarantee?'

'No, you did the right thing,' he answered quickly. 'Lumumba is a wild man, a dangerous man. But I want to be sure that you realize the gravity of your action and the risk it poses for your future as a CIA officer.'

On September 14th, Joseph Mobutu went on the radio. *'The army is installing a new 'college of commissars,'* he began slowly and matter-of-factly. *'Parliament will be closed until 1961. Joseph Kasavubu will remain as president. Patrice Lumumba has been removed and will be kept under house arrest at the residence.'*

'Furthermore, there were attempts by the Soviet Union to infiltrate the armed forces. They distributed Marxist propanganda. This cannot occur. As a result, all Soviet, Czech and Chinese diplomatic and technical personnel are being removed from this country over the next 48 hours.'

He discussed his plan to bring in young, ambitious university graduates from different tribes and regions to manage the government and to unify '*this vast country with limitless potential.*' He called them a 'college of *commissars*' – a term Denman and others hated, due to its communist etymology.

Sixteen

Late September 1960

'You know this place is still a powder keg,' Denman said to Tucci and Penderel at the popular Zoo restaurant. The restaurant was owned by a French woman and was frequented by both European diplomats and the new Congolese leadership. It had been the first restaurant to allow black Congolese to dine. Denman looked over to see Justin Bomboko, the Foreign Affairs Minister, Cyrille Adoula, a state senator and Victor Nendaka, head of State Security. They waved.

'At least not in here tonight,' Tucci laughed. 'I think we are safe. Go where the locals go, particularly if the spot is patronized by the head of state security.'

'Thank God, Mobutu has been strong,' said Penderel.

'God knows where we'd be without him. I'm glad Bomboko is involved,' he said, looking over at the table where the men seemed to be relaxed and enjoying one another. 'He's a bright guy and he's definitely pro-U.S. He's gotten to be one of Mobutu's closest allies.'

'The U.N. has been pestering Tim about elections and Lumumba getting fair treatment,' Denman added, signaling for another gin and quinine. 'The new guy, that Indian leftist, Dayal, what a pompous ass! When we met two weeks ago, he said, 'Ah, Mr. Denman. I so admire America and Americans. You make the very best air conditioners, the best refrigerators and so many fine machines. If only you concentrate on making your machines, and let us *ponder* for you.' He actually said that to me at our first meeting.'

They all cracked up as Denman put on his best Indian lilt. '*You mick de veddy best er kon-de-shun-ers.*'

'These Indians, especially the self-righteous Brahmins who get sent abroad to represent the nonaligned world, are trouble,' Tucci interjected. 'They are nothing but parasites. They should be the ones who stay home, *ponder* and fix their own shithole countries.'

'Hammarskjöld apparently likes him and thinks he can help. Dayal's no Ralph Bunche, that's for sure,' Denman continued. 'The sooner we can ensure Mr. Lumumba is isolated and away from a microphone, the sooner this country will begin to heal.'

'Yes, this country needs time to heal,' thought Penderel, remembering the private communication he received the prior evening.

Penderel had gotten a disturbing cable from Langley on September 19th marked 'PROP.' It had come from Richard Bissel, the deputy director, plans. The cable read: 'Senior officer will be arriving in Léopoldville on or around September 27th. He will identify himself as 'Ned from Paris.' Please see him as soon as possible.'

In his five years at the agency, Penderel had never gotten such a mysterious message. *That's the stuff of movies and pulp spy novels. Ian Fleming kind of stuff*, he laughed to himself. But he knew that any cable from Bissell could not be ignored.

One week later, Penderel left the embassy around 6:30 and walked down the street toward his flat. Léopoldville had regained a sense of quiet and unfinished majesty, despite the odd remnants of bashed-in shop windows that no one had yet bothered to repair.

Penderel looked forward to a small coq au vin and a glass of Chablis at Le Restaurant Cedars Élevé. Habib also had a few 'specials' that he wanted to share with him. Then, Penderel planned to rendezvous with Bomboko later that evening out at his home in the hilly suburb of Binza. Bomboko and Nendaka had become close allies, and along with Mobutu, they were the real power behind the titular throne of Joseph Kasavubu. It was good to be mobile again.

Penderel noticed a western face he'd not seen before come walking quickly towards him and his heart sank. 'I'm Ned from Paris,' the man in an ill-fitting blazer said, laughably spylike. 'I've come to give you instructions about a highly sensitive operation. Can we go to a place where we won't be observed?'

'Yes, there is a safe house six blocks from here,' answered Penderel. They split up and took different routes, meeting at a non-descript apartment on a quiet street off Blvd. de juin 30. When Ned arrived, Penderel had already unlocked the door and was sitting on the cheap sofa, covered with a green floral cotton slipcover.

'Take this,' he gestured, having pulled a wrapped package out of his valise. 'With the stuff that's in there, no one will ever know that Lumumba was assassinated.'

'Jesus H. Christ! What? Assassinate Lumumba? Who authorized this operation?'

'President Eisenhower,' Ned said. 'I wasn't there when he approved it, but Dick Bissell said that Eisenhower wanted Lumumba removed.'

Penderel lit another cigarette from the one he'd just inhaled in three drags. 'We've gotten him removed already.'

'It's your responsibility to carry out this operation, you alone. The details are up to you, but it's got to be clean – nothing that can traced back to us.' Ned had a burly build, short poorly cut hair, and a daub of moustache above his thick lip. His clothes bulged in the wrong places and he looked uncomfortable from the heat or travel. He had a southern accent, though it had an Appalachian twang. Probably West Virginia.

Ned handed over several small vials and a tube of toothpaste. 'This one,' motioning to the toothpaste, 'will cause him to come down with polio. It's up to you. No fingerprints.'

Penderel walked toward his flat, mind racing over the order to kill Lumumba. The cloak and dagger style of the interaction was comical. *Was this guy for real?* Poisoning someone's *toothpaste*? Giving him *polio*? Surely there were less dramatic methods of assuring that he didn't return to power? What if it went wrong? Then what?

He imagined a global conflagration with the Soviet Union leading the continent of Africa and the rest of the developing world against the U.S. *The headlines read 'Not-so-Bright U.S. caught in Ultrabrite Assassination Attempt.'* This was ludicrous.

Then what were the practical issues if he actually went through with it? How would I get access to his quarters? Did we have those kinds of contacts? Mobutu certainly did, but that would cause problems. *This really is a problem for the Congolese to solve for themselves. They elected him after all.*

Penderel realized he couldn't ignore the order, but decided to approach the mission cautiously, with great deliberation and careful planning. Hopefully by then, someone else would have taken on this miserable task.

He needed to be out at Binza by 8:30, which at least allowed him to drop by Habib's for a large scotch. Maybe two. Not everyday you get an order from the President to assassinate an elected head of state.

Habib nodded as Penderel came in the door of Le Restaurant Cedars Élevé. He quickly had a bus boy set up a table in the rear corner of the restaurant. 'A busy time, no?' Penderel looked up with a smile, noticing a typed list of today's specials inside the menu that Habib presented. 'You look like you need a good drink. And make sure you look at the specials.'

Penderel smiled and opened the menu. There were some interesting specials on the list. He tucked the folded slip of paper into his breast pocket.

Antoine picked Penderel up in the 1952 Volkswagen the embassy acquired during the initial crisis in July. They needed a reliable car to get around unobtrusively, although

Penderel knew they were being watched by Mobutu and the Belgians.

'Where to, Monsieur?'

'I've asked you to call me Dicky.'

He was silent, but grinning. This little game had been going on for close to a year now. Antoine was reliable and trustworthy. 'To Binza?'

'Yes.'

Penderel opened the coded note, as the breeze blew through the window. There were five names on Habib's list of specials. Three nationals in town, one of whom he'd met at a reception. Two Belgians, one of them female, he'd also met. He smiled. *I'd never, ever believed she could be turned,* he thought to himself. Habib was worth his weight in gold.

Penderel thought back to the bizarre scene with Ned from Paris. He was carrying the wrapped package in his pocket and hoped the taping was secure. *Poisoned toothpaste.* He shook his head. The CIA didn't do that kind of stuff. Fomenting coups? Sure. But overt assassinations? He didn't think the agency operated like that.

Certainly the government didn't want Lumumba in control. That had been a disaster. But the corner had been turned and Joseph Mobutu was in charge. A military guy, a rabid anti-communist the United States could do business with.

Penderel wondered if this was a test for him. Did his superiors put him in a situation to gauge his loyalty? That sounded extreme. Did Denman or Tucci know about it? Ned had said not to mention the operation to anyone, citing only Dick Bissell. *The legendary Dick Bissell of 'Plans.' The most covert of covert operatives.* Penderel needed to think about this more as the city lights and heat receded.

The quiet, leafy streets of Binza lay west of Léopoldville. The town stretched south toward Mount Ngalima, along the Lukunga River. Each Thursday evening he met with a group of Mobutu's trusted advisors that included Justin Bomboko, Victor Nendaka, and labor leader Cyrille Adoula.

This core of able young technocrats used Penderel as a sounding board for a range of timely policy and political decisions – and of course, to get funding for these initiatives. The first issue was what to do with Joseph Kasavubu, who was still president.

'Mobutu wants him fired. He's useless. He just wanders around the palace like a fat toad,' Bomboko laughed. 'He keeps demanding that new cabinet ministers get approved by him. Then he goes to take a nap.'

'Joseph can be impatient, but he is often right,' Penderel

countered. 'But sacking Kasavubu will only play into the U.N.'s hands. You want that arrogant little Indian in your face? I can assure you he will be.'

Adoula answered, 'I agree that Joseph needs to calm down. Without Kasavubu, we have no legitimacy. Mr. Dayal thinks that he is our babysitter. He's more English than the snobbiest of the public school boys I met in the British diplomatic service.

'He's a racist, too,' Cyrille Adoula added. 'He made some wisecracks about apes in the jungle.'

'Forget him,' interjected Penderel. 'Let's keep our eye on the subject. Why don't we convince our dear army friend to work with a council of associates? Let's not call then commissars. Denman hates the term. The U.S. can help financially support the council. They can choose cabinet officials for our President. That should achieve our goal, no?'

'Perhaps,' said Bomboko. 'I will speak to him in the morning. I suspect the sweetener will be appreciated.'

'What else?' Penderel asked.

'Well, we have been talking amongst ourselves that Mr. Lumumba should be arrested,' the director of the *Sûreté Nationale du Congo* suggested. 'He no longer deserves a pulpit from which to carry on.'

'First, you would need to attack and dismantle his U.N. security detail,' Penderel replied. 'Do you know what that would do?'

'Yes, yes, yes,' Adoula answered laughing. 'More lecturing from the little Brahmin … and more U.N. troops.'

'And a move to reinstate Lumumba and immediately hold elections,' Penderel answered, enjoying the breeze and long drag of a Chesterfield. 'Everyone needs to be more patient. There will be a right time to deal with Mr. Lumumba. Rome was not built in a day.'

With that, they shook hands and adjourned for the evening.

Penderel was relaxed driving back into town. It had been a strange day, but it ended well. His group of commissars had gelled into a practical, calm cadre of governors in a short time. Léopoldville was mostly peaceful and the military had regained order in the city.

The names Habib had provided were surprising, but helpful. It was critical to get information from different sources if only to corroborate other intelligence.

Nearly a year into his job, Penderel felt like he was a

major contributor for good in this first posting abroad. It made him feel proud.

He folded the list of specials and returned them to his coat packet. Then he felt the small wrapped package he'd been given by Ned. It felt dirty and evil, like a biblical temptation. He couldn't think about it tonight. He was proud of what he had accomplished.

Seventeen

October 1960

Penderel spent most of his time since independence developing additional contacts. With the chaos, nothing was ever as it seemed. Habib Khouri was his first source and he had an amazing ability to eavesdrop on his patrons. The influx of Soviet-backed advisors over the winter was stemmed with the Mobutu coup, so most of the newer intelligence efforts were directed at the Belgians who frequented his restaurant.

Delvaux was too slick and experienced ever to reveal anything of real value, but most of the Belgian military advisors were loud and indiscreet after a few brandies after dinner.

The secession of Katanga created problems that the

U.S. had little control over. The United Nations and central government made a lot of noise about re-engagement, but there was little anyone could do to force reintegration. Tshombe and his Lunda tribe and security forces had free rein to govern the territory as they saw fit. This started with the minority Baluba tribe in northern Katanga.

It was rumored that the ongoing 'disagreements' with the Baluba tribe had resulted in nearly 60,000 deaths since independence. The work was quietly carried out by the Katanga gendarmerie, composed mostly of white mercenaries.

Penderel had little sympathy for the Baluba cause. It would just be another Congolese group that would fuck things up. But he disagreed with the outright contempt Tsombe showed for his fellow Katangans.

In truth, Penderel understood very little about what exactly was going on in Katanga. He thought back to his initial impressions – *a professional, well-oiled machine.* But he had little else in terms of understanding their operational thinking and long-term strategy beyond retaining power and control.

Still, there were still individuals who were willing to cooperate with the United States completely. But Penderel would never have guessed that one of them would be Beryl Reader.

'So, Dicky,' she said, over the phone. 'I've been watching this for three months and don't like where it is headed. I want to help you.'

'How so?' answered Penderel.

'Meet me at The Regina. I'll explain.'

Penderel had not expected this. He knew that they were sexually attracted to one another, though he never imagined it would come to fruition. She was a fantasy and an object of desire to be lusted after from a distance. But she said *I want to help you*? That was an odd come-on, he thought.

Penderel knocked on the door of room 213 at The Regina. A light rain had begun to fall and the clattery sound of drops added to the eerie, secretive atmosphere. He pushed the door open. Beryl was sitting in a chair, smoking a cigarette. She had on a polka-dot dress and her visage in the dimmed incandescent light was languid. She looked across the room at Penderel. 'Oh God I've been thinking about this all day long,' she murmured. 'Come here.'

Penderel walked over to Beryl, offering his hand as she stood up. Her hands were cool and firm as he embraced her. Her back was muscular and she in turn squeezed his torso closer as they kissed, almost violently. Beryl looked up from the tight hold, smiled and closed her eyes, as she tucked herself into his ribcage, locking herself onto him.

Penderel smelled her exotic perfume, the scent he remembered from Elysium. This was finally the moment, though his mind was racing. *Slow down, slow down*, he tried telling himself, but he couldn't.

Beryl opened her eyes, looked up, grabbed Penderel's shirt, and pulled him toward her. They began to laugh as Penderel tripped, trying to disrobe and kick off his shoes. The one chair in the hotel room tipped over, creating a loud *thump*. They howled at their adolescent clumsiness, but it made them even more frenetic. *Slow, down, slow down.* Both naked, they sprung into bed, young lovers intoxicated with each others' bodies after months of anticipation.

Immediately Beryl had Penderel on his back, stradding him in the opposite direction, as they groped each other; lips, tongues and fingers in constant movement and intersection. It continued for fifteen minutes, before he eased onto her. Urgently, she climbed on top of him, moving back and forth, quicker and quicker, firmer and firmer before climaxing. Exhausted, they collapsed into a satiated trance.

'Oh, thank you, thank you,' she murmured huskily. 'That was marvelous. I had at least two orgasms.' She was sitting up, smiling, reaching over to the bedside table for a cigarette.

'I'm flattered. I can admit to one, but it was a very long and satisfying one,' answered Penderel. He was still in an ecstatic stupor, not wanting it to go away.

'I've missed this for twelve years,' Beryl said slowly, before howling out loud with release and delight.

'*What?*' Penderel blurted. Beryl was sitting up, giggling and babbling cheerily.

'It's a long story, but let's just say my husband's equipment doesn't work very well.' She smiled and clapped her hands. 'There, I said it! I've wanted to tell someone that for so long. Finally. Thank you, Richard Penderel. Thank you!'

Penderel lay on his back, stunned, not knowing what to say, though he knew her admission was honest. 'Wow! That is one thing I never imagined.'

She shimmied her head onto his chest, watching it thrust up and down as his heartbeat slowly returned to normal. 'You're a handsome man. I want more of you.'

'Seems we've both been underutilized,' Penderel answered. 'And you, Beryl Reader, are a stunningly attractive woman.'

'Thank you so much,' she said blissfully, eyes bright and face aglow. She laughed like a young girl. 'Does it show that I'm out of practice?' she sat up, blond hair messy and tangled, like a feral child. 'I hope to hell so.

'I have something that I want to discuss with you,' she began, excitedly. 'It's something I've given a lot of thought to. Would you like some champagne?' A bottle of Tattinger sat chilled in a bucket.

Penderel was dumbfounded. He had just had passionate sex with a woman he'd fantasized about over the past eleven months. It just happened. She was so real, so passionate; so honest. And she was there, talking to him.

Beryl's voice and cadence lowered, as she began to speak, measured, almost monotone, though her body posture was still coiled and athletic.

'I want the United States to take a far more active role in helping this country. You have finally moved from the sidelines by putting Mobutu in charge. That is a good first step. But you need to do more to ensure this country has a future.

'I've learned much that disturbs me. The Belgians will stop at nothing to maintain their influence and control. That starts and ends with Katanga. I trust you, though I'm not sure yet that I trust the United States. I'm not sure at all about your boss, Mr. Denman. That is what I want to talk about.'

She paused, putting her cigarette out, taking a sip of champagne. She sat in the bed naked and cross-legged, unconcerned about her visible crotch. 'Can I trust you?'

'Yes, absolutely,' said Penderel, mind still reeling.

'I'd like to propose getting together on a regular basis. I don't want money. That's the least of my worries. I like your company. In exchange, I will provide information about things I've learned. That's all.'

Penderel watched as she put her glass on the table. She turned and sighed. 'All I need is to have a mirror so I can see us when we are together. It sounds strange, but I have a lifetime of lovemaking to catch up on. Seeing, hearing, smelling, tasting and touching is what I want from you. But watching amplifies the experience for me. Does this make sense?'

'Sort of.' Penderel was having a hard time taking all of this in.

'Also, you cannot reveal who I am. To anyone. You're to refer to me as a Belgian woman. That should be easy. There are a lot of discontented ones in town. I don't trust your boss, but I trust your government will make good decisions based on my information. If anyone finds out about this, particularly my husband, we'll both be killed. After, we've been tortured.'

'I understand,' Penderel answered, though he was still feeling his way through all of this. He trusted her, though he suspected no one else would. *Watch that bird* was Denman's refrain. 'But why do you want to risk it?'

'Dicky, I love this country and believe it will only succeed if our native population is allowed to rule. There will be setbacks and mistakes, but democracy is not just a privilege for white intellectuals. I believe the United States is the only country inherently good enough to help us and to ensure this country, eventually, will be free.

'There are things we must do that are right and necessary, but are not safe or smart. I guess I'm roping you into my suicide mission for the Congolese people. After all, you're a war hero, Dicky. Aren't you?'

Eighteen

Early November 1960

'You're not going to believe this,' Ambassador Timberlake said one morning. 'For some strange reason, the USIA is sponsoring an African tour for Louis Armstrong. One of his stops is in Elisabethville.'

'You mean Louis Armstrong is playing in the capital of the so-called State of Katanga, a political entity that the U.S. doesn't recognize?' Penderel answered, laughing. 'Given everything else I've observed over the past year, that seems about right. Only person better would be Screaming Jay Hawkins.'

'Ah, the beauty of diplomacy! OK, Mr. Jazzman, do you want to join George, Leon and me? We need an excuse to meet with Tshombe anyway.'

'We're not going to get much out of Tshombe, but I love jazz,' said Penderel. 'Saw him play in New York right after the war. He puts on one helluva show.'

Timberlake, Tucci, Denman and Penderel arrived in Elisabethville in the early afternoon in time for a late lunch. Tshombe and a delegation of Katanga officials met them at the airport, with a band playing and lots of press cameras flashing. 'This is the one thing I knew would happen. Legitimacy in the eyes of the world,' Timberlake grumbled.

'When the saint goes marching in,' laughed Tucci. 'I want to be in that number.'

The luncheon at Tshombe's palace was a predictably grand affair. It was attended by numerous Katangan ministers and their wives, the Bivers, Beryl Reader, a few unidentified Rhodesians and of course, Louis Armstrong and his wife.

'Just don't say anything that implies that we recognize Katanga,' Tucci whispered in Timberlake's ear. 'But you can address him as 'Monsieur le President,' since he is president of the province.'

'Thank you, chief of protocol,' Timberlake cracked, before standing to give a toast. Penderel was lucky enough to sit between Louis Armstrong and Beryl Reader.

'So, Mr. Armstrong, I've been a fan of yours forever. You must get exhausted from all this travel. How is the tour going?' Penderel asked.

'It's been terrific, so far,' Armstrong answered. He pulled out two little packets of Swiss Kriss, an herbal laxative. 'Sometimes the travel is tough and hard on my system. This keeps me regular. Satch says 'leave it all behind ya.'

Penderel broke out laughing, as others across the table looked on. Armstrong continued, 'This is my secret to a long and healthy life,' holding packets up for all to see. The bright lime and Kelly green packets were scattered across the table, as the stuffy guests smiled anxiously. 'These are *all natural.* I use them *every day.*'

Armstrong looked up and whispered to Penderel, 'Do you know where I can get a few sticks of gage? It helps me relax before shows.'

'Let me look into it, sir,' Penderel answered. His role as a diplomat required many skills, so procuring marijuana for an American celebrity was just another subversive operation to accomplish before the evening show.

Whether it was the Swiss Kriss or the high-test marijuana, Louis Armstrong put on a spectacular show. He played for two hours, including three encores, leaving the skeptical jazz fans in the audience converted. Penderel managed to retain a little of the gage for his own purposes.

Penderel was a booze man at heart, but a few times after the war, he tried smoking marijuana on visits to jazz clubs. There was something perversely pleasureable about being a decorated war hero and doing something illegal. And he reasoned marijuana was not illegal here anyway.

'Plane leaves at 7 a.m. with or without you,' Ambassador Timberlake called out, as they parted the table. 'I'm off to bed and I encourage you all to do the same.' They strolled out into the cool November night, extolling the talents of Satchmo and his orchestra.

'Well, who's up for a nightcap at the hotel?' asked Tucci. Both Denman and Penderel begged off, citing tiredness and work to do. Tucci looked up at Penderel, not used to excuses for one last brandy. 'You too?'

'Yea, me too. But I'll take a cab back to the hotel with you.'

'Let's go.'

Penderel went up his room and immediately called Beryl. 'It was a bit awkward back there. I wondered if you'd like a nightcap?'

'You're funny. Do you mean do I want to meet you for a rendezvous?' She was silent for a few seconds. 'Yes,' she said with certainty. 'I've been fantasizing about it all night. Timothy is away. Where?'

'Number 34 Avenue Wangaree. Around the backside, along the alleyway. The door will be unlocked.'

Penderel quietly went out the back entrance and quietly hailed a cab to the Hotel de Bruxelles. He paid the driver, got out and walked around the corner to Avenue Wangareee where the Embassy kept a small, non-descript flat. It was rarely used. He unlocked the door, tossed the key on the table and waited nervously.

The flat was sparsely furnished with a single bedroom and a sitting area. Over the past three weeks, Beryl had told Penderel about a plot by the Belgians to assassinate Patrice Lumumba.. Many of the details were sketchy, though the plan involved senior members of the Katangan and Belgian governments. Beryl had also told him that Tshombe had no intention of ever reuniting with the rest of the Congo.

But even the excitement of her trove of intelligence didn't compare to the intensity of making love to her. Penderel felt like a teenager, needy, reckless and wanton. She was so vital and alive.

'Want to try some gage?' he laughed, finding the smelly marijuana cigarette in his shirt pocket, after they made love.

'What's that?' she asked, sitting up in the bed.

'The stuff that makes Louis Armstrong sing and play his horn so well. Marijuana.' Penderel uncreased the small paper bag and a pungent, sweet odor permeated the room.

Her eyes brightened and she laughed again, free and fulfilled. 'Why not? I've never tried it. It's really been a night for experimentation. They call what we did something, right? There's a name for it?'

'I believe in French it is called 'soixante-neuf.'

Beryl and Penderel lay back in bed, sharing a misshapen hand-rolled joint of gage, giggling like schoolchildren.

Nineteen

Early November 1960

'So is John Kennedy going to be your next President?' Victor Nendaka asked. It was nearing midnight two days before the U.S. elections. Only Bomboko and Nendaka remained up, as the others from the Binza group had headed home.

'He surely would be better than the old general,' Bomboko answered. 'He's young and idealistic. He wants to change the world.'

'We won't know until morning,' Penderel answered. 'I prefer the continuity of the Republican Party. You of all people shouldn't knock the effectiveness of a military man in place of youth and charisma.'

Everyone chuckled. 'But what to do with our man of charisma?' Nendaka asked. 'This U.N. protection can't go on. Lumumba is still agitating and making speeches. He's got the support from Ghana, Guinea and the whole Soviet bloc. Rumor has it that the Soviets are back, smuggling arms to his supporters. There have been skirmishes in the north of Katanga.'

'Yes, Mr. Penderel,' Bomboko added. 'I hear rumors about white military guests operating in the east? Any truth?'

'I can't speak to that, Justin,' replied Penderel. 'But we do agree that Monsieur Tshombe has the right to tamp down on dissent and leftist guerrilla activity in his province.'

'It is dangerous to allow that to go on,' Nendaka answered. 'Our military is too weak to have a meaningful presence there.'

'I hate to see us killing one another,' Cyrille Adoula added. 'But this is Tshombe's problem to manage. He desires autonomy. That isn't free.'

'Keeping a lid on the pro-Lumumbists is essential right now,' said Nendaka. 'We must deal with the most pressing crisis of the moment. But it would be nice to look ahead.'

Penderel gazed at Bomboko and Nendaka. Over the past two months, they had grown and matured as leaders. Mobutu was not there that evening, but there was a silent acceptance of the need for covert foreign military support.

They needed to stay in the background and not draw too much attention to themselves. It was just one of many interrelated challenges, he thought to himself, throwing back the remainder of his watered-down scotch.

Penderel looked out the car's back window as Antoine rumbled through the silent neighborhood of Binza. It was nearly midnight and the air clung with a sweet sticky aroma. It smelled like marijuana. He would never think again of marijuana without thinking of Beryl Reader. That night listening to Louis Armstrong, having sex, smoking gage and giggling. It was so memorable, as he recreated every move, gesture and conversation from that marvelous, magical evening.

There was no one on the road, except for a street sweeper. He waved, wondering who might be out at this time of night. Penderel lit another cigarette and offered one to Antoine.

'So what do you think of this new government?'

'I'm very happy,' Antoine answered, exhaling. 'It's peaceful here. People are back out on the streets. The markets are full again. Life's back to normal.'

'Yes, it is peaceful,' answered Penderel, looking out of the window. The outskirts of Léopoldville came upon them quickly. There were pockets of young men hanging about, some laughing, others moving, others working. But the sounds were happy, like schoolkids in recess. The squeaky brakes of garbage trucks punctuated the stillness.

This was a big, complex city with the rhythms of a twenty-four hour cycle. Soon the produce would be coming in on trucks or oxcarts. He hoped that peace would last. The stopgap measure of installing Mobutu had been necessary and was working.

What to do with Lumumba? Penderel wondered. Since Mobutu's coup in September, Lumumba had been kept under house arrest at the Prime Minister's residence. He had been allowed to move about under protection from the United Nations, but it wasn't a long-term solution. It made him think about his own mission that he'd yet to act on.

What to do with the little pouch that Ned from Paris had given him? It remained in the top drawer of the dresser in his flat, tucked behind his boxer shorts and navy socks. There had been cryptic follow-up about status and planning.

Penderel wondered again if Denman or Tucci knew about this. He had to assume so, but neither had ever mentioned it. He justified his lack of action on circumstances and security. No one could know and he'd yet to identify a method of achieving the desired result without anyone knowing.

Maybe this was their test for me? Soldiers carry out orders.

Penderel had spent his life doing that. *But this was different. It had to be executed perfectly and the conditions were far from perfect. Everyone understood that, so maybe the test was one of judgment rather than loyalty?*

The notion that the United States planned to poison the deposed prime minister of a sovereign nation and ally bothered Penderel. It was clunky and amateurish. Not something he associated with the CIA.

He admired his fellow agents – their professionalism, their fairness, even their idealism, but this little pouch signified an evil, stupid cancer in the system. How isolated it was, he didn't know. It had brought an unfamiliar tenor to the job he'd been recently quite proud of doing.

Penderel, Tucci and Denman sat around the embassy the next afternoon. It appeared that John Kennedy had narrowly defeated Vice President Richard Nixon. No one knew what it would mean for U.S. policy toward Congo. Initial indications weren't great. Kennedy had promised to work more closely with the U.N. in Africa and other newly independent countries.

'Don't pay it any mind,' Denman said to Tucci and Penderel. 'Kennedy has his own list of priorities -- Viet Nam, the Soviets and the Cubans. The last thing he wants is this place to get on the front page again. If we can keep the Congo out of the headlines, no one will care what goes on.'

'But we have to do something about Lumumba, sir,' Tucci interjected. 'He can't just sit under house arrest forever. He's a distraction to all the good work the commissars have been achieving. Just when something good happens, he makes an incendiary speech. At a minimum, we should turn him over to the Congolese. This is their problem to solve.'

'We need to be patient,' Denman answered. 'We just need to be patient. And stop calling them commissars, dammit!'

Twenty

Late November 1960

'I wanted to relay something that I just discovered,' Habib said. 'It may be of interest.'

'What is it?' replied Penderel. It was nearing midnight and the restaurant was empty. Habib poured a brandy and sat down at the rear table nearest the kitchen.

'I spent the last Thursday over in Brazzaville with Noor and the kids. I'd forgotten what a lovely place it is. It's so different from here. Reminds me of the neighborhoods in Beirut. No grand boulevards, just low-lying stucco buildings with green tin roofs. There are cafes with zinc tabletops and walled gardens dripping with bougainvillea and hibiscus. It has a true feel of France in the tropics. Maybe I should have settled there?' He looked up, smiled wistfully and continued speaking.

'Well, we had lunch at the Café des Pais. It's like this, only more casual, run by a Syrian couple I know. The view looks out over the Stanley Pool. We had fresh baguettes and a delicious river fish with chilis dish called *maboke.*'

'Sounds delightful,' replied Penderel.

'I noticed a group of men sitting in a back room of the café. I few of the men looked familiar. Belgians I had seen around Leo. Can't place their names. I've seen one of them in the restaurant, a Frenchman, I think his name is Denard. Looks like military.'

'Yes,' said Penderel. 'He's known to be a mercenary. Fought in Algeria. And he also tried to assassinate the French Prime Minister in 1954. He's crazy.'

'They were speaking English. There was a large, thick-necked man too, who seemed to be directing the conversation. His accent was South African, maybe Kenyan? I'm not good with these different English accents.'

'Interesting,' said Penderel. 'Any other faces you recognize?'

'There was one man, who looked out of place. I've seen him at the restaurant once. He was too well dressed to be at a seaside cafe. He stuck out, like a dandy. His spoke in both French and English, but the French was Belgian-accented. Very upper crust accent.'

'Huh,' thought Penderel. *I guess the Elyseum crowd is on the move.* 'Did you hear anything?'

'Not really. I was just using the toilette. But when I passed by, the conversation stopped and they fiddled with their wine, looking around. Same when I returned to my table. I don't think they paid me any mind. Or hope they didn't.'

'That's all very interesting,' said Penderel. 'Thank you. I don't know what it means.' *Contingency plans are afoot.*

On the night of November 27th, an enormous thunderstorm hit Léopoldville, dropping six inches of rain in a little over three hours and lighting up the evening skies. Most of the Congolese army surrounding the palace ran for cover, wherever they could avoid the torrents of water, booms of thunder and frequent lightning strikes.

The sudden and violent power of weather always loomed, like a guerilla army, striking hard and unexpectedly. From the sky, the endless landmass seemed sleepy and monotonous. But up close, it was angry and unpredictable, much like its inhabitants. Weather, like the people could be docile and beautiful, until a spark is lit and everything instantly explodes. During the storm, Patrice Lumumba slipped away from house arrest at his residence in a black car.

'How did this happen?' asked an enraged Mobutu to his inner circle the next morning.

'The rain was very bad,' answered Bomboko. 'His allies have been waiting for the right moment to spring him. I suspect the U.N. was involved.'

'He's must be headed to Stanleyville,' Nendaka announced. 'This is ideal. He's on the run. It's not like he can hop on a plane. He'll have to take cars and ferries, just like everyone else. He has limited protection now.'

'You know he is clever, Victor,' Mobutu said. 'But he will give himself away. He's too vain to travel quietly. The first town he comes to, he'll want to give a speech.'

'The *Force Publique* and our internal security services are at our disposal,' Nendaka added. 'We will have our man within days.'

'Yes,' Mobutu said. 'It is important that he not get to Stanleyville. I know this man's ambitions. He wants to regain power and that is where his political base has retreated. That's where the Soviets are and where the AK-47s are coming from. Please Victor, please reassure me that he will be caught and punished before he causes this nation any more harm.'

'Yes, you have my word,' Nendaka answered slowly, staring into the non-blinking eyes of the forceful Chief of the Army.

'Justin-Marie,' said Mobutu. 'We probably don't need to involve any of our foreign friends in this activity. Patrice Lumumba is our problem. We may disagree with our secessionist brothers, but we share the goal of ridding Congo of him.'

'Yes, I think this escape will be a good thing after all,' answered Bomboko.

'Mr. Penderel, Justin Bomboko is on the line. Can you take it?'

'Yes, of course.'

'I guess congratulations are in order,' Penderel began. 'You captured him and no one was killed.'

'Yes, it was a successful mission. We are all satisfied. Except of course, for the press.' Nendaka's deputy cabled his boss on the morning of December 1st at Lodi, on the left bank of the Sankuru River in South Kasai.

'LUMUMBA CAPTURÉE' read the simple message.

But Patrice Lumumba's return to captivity to a base north of Léopoldville was anything but successful. In full view of the assembled international press, the *Sûreté*

Nationale du Congo had beaten the former Prime Minister with batons and chiccotes.

‘’The press, yes, that was what I wanted to discuss with you,’ said Penderel slowly, anger building. ‘Why in hell would Victor’s men beat him up in full view of all the foreign press corps? It was really stupid.’

‘Yes, it was unfortunate,’ answered Bomboko. ‘A mistake that won’t be repeated. Victor knows that.’

‘Going forward, you must make sure he understands that,’ said Penderel firmly. ‘Now pictures are being transmitted all over the world. People will think that you are blood-thirsty savages.’

‘I resent that characterization, Mr. Penderel,’ Bomboko answered sharply, hurt. ‘Whenever we do something excessive, the West says we’re ‘savages.’ People in this country understand savagery -- enslavement, cutting off hands. Now that is savagery. We do not need lectures.’

‘Yes, Justin-Marie,’ said Penderel. ‘That is fair and I apologize.’ Penderel was angry for losing his cool and insulting one of the young bright leaders in the country. He took a deep breath and quietly exhaled.

‘The sooner we can permanently get Lumumba off stage, the better for everyone,’ Bomboko answered calmly. ‘He is being transferred to an elite brigade camp in

Thysville this afternoon. That will keep him out of the spotlight.'

'I agree, but remember, that's where the problems started. We don't need another uprising or escape.'

'Yes, I understand. It won't happen. Mr. Mobutu has assured us.'

Penderel's mind was reeling. The pictures of the beating on the television stuck in his mind. There were things about Lumumba that Penderel admired. He cared enough for his country that he is willing to lay down his life in support of a higher ideal -- freedom from tyranny and the ability for his countrymen to pursue happiness. *If only he could work within the system.*

'Will you pour me some champagne, darling?'

Penderel returned from the bathroom and walked over to the refrigerator. Other than the mirror that he tried not to look into, Beryl requested a bottle of chilled Tattinger that afternoon.

'Of course. And a Gitane?'

'So I expect you want to know about what the Belgians plan to do with Lumumba?' Beryl sat up in the bed, naked, aggravated and impatient. 'Thank you,' she said as he handed her the glass. The expression on her face was solemn. He lit her cigarette.

'Or what his countrymen plan to do for that matter?' Penderel answered, putting on a bathrobe and sitting on the bed. 'The poor dumb son-of-a-bitch is going to get killed anyway.'

'You're right. From what I've heard, the Belgians are actively advising the gendarmerie in Katanga. I've told you about Barracuda, Count d'Aspremont's operation. Unlike you, they don't pretend with niceties.'

The whole group regularly meets over in Brazzaville. The Count, Marlière, Bob Denard, and several others from the army. The only reason he isn't already dead is that he's been under house arrest. Now you have this information, what does the United States plan to do? You promised a fair outcome.'

Penderel looked at her. She was taking a deep drag of her cigarette and motioning for more champagne. He'd also heard about these meetings in Brazzaville from Habib. Denman had promised to try to convince the Belgians and new government to deal with Lumumba humanely. So far, it had been handled that way.

'Those pictures from his capture were pretty gruesome,' Penderel said, stroking her back. She had tanned, freckled skin from too much time outside in the sun.

'Yeah, it made me ill too,' Beryl said, stubbing her cigarette out. She turned toward Penderel and stared at him intensely. 'Would you put your arm around me?' He put his glass down and sat back on the pillow. Beryl put her face on his bare chest and ran her hand along his side, pausing to squeeze and caress his shoulders.

Penderel still had a young man's build for a forty-year old with horrible eating habits. They lay silently in the bed, slowly rubbing each other, as the occasional honk of a horn on the street reminded them of where they were.

'You know the reason I came to you was to get the U.S. to make the new government treat Lumumba with respect and dignity. You are the only counterweight to effect a decent, civilized outcome for the Congo. Left to others, including my monster of a husband, this place will be a never-ending war zone.'

Penderel looked ahead at the oversized mirror in the intricately carved mahogany, art deco frame. This time she wasn't looking ahead, but silently resting her head, eyes shut on his chest. He closed his eyes, thinking. *Can the U.S. be a force for good here?* He wasn't sure.

Penderel drifted off to sleep, as the regularity of her breathing calmed and relaxed him. A gentle rain began on the tin roof outside, clanking like a pinball machine. He felt her hands rub his neck and shoulder as they had turned to spoon. A siren went by outside the window and woke both of them. Penderel sat up startled. It was just 3 p.m. They had only been asleep for fifteen minutes.

'It's so nice lying here next to you,' she said. 'I miss cuddling.'

Penderel smiled. He had too. Her alternate bravado and vulnerability intrigued him. Her motivations and terms – intimacy in exchange for secrets that could lead to a better outcome for her country – were noble, if not wreckless and treasonous. It would probably get both of them killed. Could Penderel trust Denman and the organization he worked for?

Beryl got out of bed and walked naked to the window. She was still fit, although her body had begun to sag into her butt. She turned with a smile, after grabbing another cigarette from the table. 'You know they are planning to kill Lumumba? Don't you?'

'It will be hard to do, now that he is back in captivity,' Penderel said reassuringly. 'The U.N. won't allow it to happen.'

'He'll escape again. They will ensure that happens. Then they will take him to the east where they will murder him and dispose of his body. The plan is set. The timing is all that remains unknown.'

'Are you certain?'

'Yes … and there will be substantial assistance from outsiders. Mind you, nothing that anyone will ever prove.'

Twenty-One

January 1961

'Happy New Year,' Denman toasted. 'It's got to be a better one than we just finished.'

The beginning of 1961 was a continuation of 1960. Lumumba remained a prisoner at Thysville. The Congolese army was still restive and demanding better pay. The world press had become increasingly sympathetic to Lumumba, as Mobutu showed no signs of restoring the parliament as he had promised. This sequence of events had turned into a slow-motion disaster -- a slog that had no finish line.

'You're not kidding,' answered Penderel soberly. What Beryl had relayed about the plot to murder Lumumba had been eating at him for three weeks. She was so certain, as though it had already happened.

Penderel tried to gently raise the issue with his boss, but was cautious. Could the U.S. be involved? After all, somebody had come all the way from Langley to order him to poison Lumumba.

And what about Beryl? She was married after all, so their affair was wrong … and dangerous. Her husband would beat her to a pulp if he found out and probably kill both of them too. But he had fallen in love with her. She had brought passion, idealism and danger into his life. She was the first person to teach him to ask 'why?'

There was something about her spirit that he wanted for himself, something all the missions and medals never stirred in him. He went *on missions*; she lived *with a mission. What a way to live!* It was a feeling he'd never experienced before. She was a person of great integrity, willing to put her life on the line not to win medals, but to make a difference. He wanted to escape and settle down with her.

Back at the mission, Penderel took the call. He hung up the phone with a sigh. 'That was Bomboko,' he announced to Tucci and Denman. 'The Thysville garrison just mutinied.' A wave of nausea swept across his body: he sensed this was the first announcement of many bad ones that had been foretold.

'They want a pay raise,' Penderel continued.

'Jesus, this is how this whole mess started in the first place!' said Tucci.

'Nendaka, Mobutu and he are headed down to try to get things settled. Unclear if Lumumba has escaped again,' answered Penderel.

'All three? Huh? Seems overkill to have all of them there. Something's up,' Tucci replied.

Denman was smoking a cigarette and didn't speak.

Later that afternoon, Bomboko called Penderel again. He relayed that the mutiny was under control and Lumumba was back in captivity. *Lumumba is being sent to another prison in Katanga. No need to be concerned. We've got it under control.*

Penderel knew exactly what this meant. It was how Beryl had described what would happen. *They will take him to the east where they will murder him and dispose of his body. The plan is set. The timing is all that remains unknown. And there will be substantial assistance from outsiders.*

'That was all he said?' Tucci asked. 'Odd. Bomboko and the others usually want to hash out all of the options. Agree, something's fishy.'

Denman stood up and wrinkled his face. 'They're finally going to do something about him. And they're leaving us out of the fray. Considerate of them.'

Penderel knew that this was coming. Still, what likely lay ahead sickened him: more beatings and finally a brutal execution somewhere, sometime soon. Lumumba would simply be a man who disappeared.

'But aren't we providing some tacit approval of this?' Penderel asked. 'What do we tell Langley?'

'Funny, we got a cable from State this morning denying our request for funds to pay off the officers of a key garrison in the east threatening to put Lumumba back in power,' Denman answered. 'They want the new administration to make these kinds of decisions. And early indications are that Kennedy will take a softer line towards Lumumba to appease the fucking U.N.'

'So it doesn't behoove anyone for us to force unwanted information on either State or Langley right now?' Tucci asked.

Denman sighed and quietly spoke. 'The truth of the matter is that our commission friends are not asking our opinion on anything regarding the future of Patrice Lumumba. In fact, they are specifically *not* doing that. That really should satisfy everyone.'

'Do we think there is any outside assistance? They've left us out, but what about the Belgians?' asked Penderel, trying to see how his boss might fill empty spaces. The answers Denman had offered so far gave him a chill.

'Good question,' answered Denman slowly. 'And one I'm not keen to dig around on too much. If the Belgians are part of any plot to eliminate Mr. Lumumba, then that is their business. The United States does not benefit from any association with this. If anything happens to him, the Soviets and the U.N. will blame us anyway.'

'Odd, I just remember a conversation last year with our boss, Mr. Dillon,' said Penderel. 'He said, 'seems we should let those parties take the lead. Nothing gained by publicly sticking our nose under the tent.'

Denman smiled. 'Yes, Prescott Dillon is a very smart man. A man who understands contingency planning.'

Timothy Reader was spending a very busy January, mostly away from Elisabethville and his wife Beryl. Count d'Aspremont had started his Operation Barricuda on December 2nd, the day after Lumumba was recaptured. He bothered Reader everyday with picayune logistical questions. Reader didn't mind d'Aspremont, though he viewed him as lazy and imperious. He often thought he would remind 'The Count' -- as he called him behind his back -- that Moise Tshombe paid his wages, not him, a faded aristocrat who needed something to do.

That d'Aspremont was Belgium's Minister of African Affairs amused him – Belgium only had two colonies to 'minister' to and the other – Ruanda-Urundi, a former German territory, the size of Israel – was given to it following World War I. D'Aspremont was a pompous ass whom he dreaded having to host at Elyseum. But Biver always prevailed with his argument about shared interests.

'Timothy,' the Count's unmistakable voice said over the line. 'He's on the way, along with two other revolutionary communists. Flight left this morning. Should be in Elisabethville by early afternoon. They're being punished as we speak.'

Reader was angry. 'Harold, the last time you put him on an airplane and beat the hell out of him, the international press corps was there to record it. Talk to Tshombe and whoever else. No press, no U.N.'

'I'll see what I can do,' d'Aspremont answered. 'The plans are set?'

'Yes, they are,' said Reader. 'We'll take him up to Villa Brouwe for questioning. I know President Tshombe would like some answers. Your detail will be there, correct?'

'Yes, both Captain Julien Gat and Police Commissioner Frans Verscheure will be there.'

'Good,' Reader answered. 'There can't be any screw-ups this time.'

'It will be done with Belgian professionalism and efficiency,' d'Aspremont replied.

Reader stared at the phone, shaking his head as he hung up. 'Fucking idiot.'

The flight arrived from Thysville in the late afternoon. The trio was bloody, stumbling, and handcuffed as they disembarked, just as Reader had feared. He shook his head. 'What is it with these stupid people? Someone will ask questions or notice the blood on the plane.'

But there was no press corps, only the planned Katanga police and Belgian military awaiting the flight. A white armored van pulled up to the tarmac. Three uniformed officers quickly got out, covered the three prisoners with a canvas tarp, before tossing them into the rear cargo bay.

The van roared off north along the one-lane highway, arriving at sunset at a poorly tended, remote villa, owned by a Belgian who skipped the country six months earlier. Several cabinet ministers and President Tshombe were already there. The officers stripped away the tarp, revealing Lumumba and his two associates. They were bare-chested and barefoot, dressed only in their trousers and vests.

'So this is what democracy has brought us?' Lumumba asked loudly and defiantly to the assembled group. But he was staring directly at Moise Tshombe and his interior minister, Godfried Munongo. Lumumba had lacerations and bruises over the visible parts of his body and was limping as though he had a broken leg. Still, his voice was firm and certain.

'The Belgians have taught us to torture one another. That is their legacy. The others here,' he said pointing to the assemblage of twenty Belgian troops and policemen, 'are not a surprise. You did not give this country a chance. We could have been a great land, a beacon for all of Africa, but instead you are venal and greedy like our slavemasters.'

Lumumba glared at Tshombe, dressed in a sharp, tailored grey worsted suit. His left eye was swollen shut.

'Take him away, please,' said Tshombe. 'Our new beginning must begin now.'

Police Commissioner Verscheure loaded the three prisoners back into the van. The four-car convoy headed east along an unpaved road, away from the villa. It was dark outside, a moonless, overcast night. The van pulled into a clearing twenty minutes later. Several soldiers were there, digging a large hole beside an enormous baobab tree.

'Get out,' said the Commisioner, 'get out now.' Verschuere removed the handcuffs from Lumumba and the two others. 'Walk ahead,' he commanded.

'Vous allez nous tuer, n'est-ce pas?' Lumumba asked.

'Yes.'

Lumumba smiled, standing in the clearing. The baobab, five feet in diameter rose before them, like an altar – large, intricate, with a sense of power and permanance. Lumumba wasn't afraid, though he took three short breaths to steady himself.

'Would any of you like some time to pray?' asked Captain Gat. The three looked up and silently shook their heads 'no.'

'OK, Mr. Okito,' said the Commissioner, pointing. 'You are first.' The first firing squad consisting of two soldiers and two policemen stepped forward as Gat led Okito toward the large tree. He yelled, 'I want my wife and two children in Léopoldville to be taken care of.'

'We're in Katanga, not in Leo,' was the answer from the Police Commissioner. A hail of bullets from twelve feet rang out and the former vice president of the Senate was dead. His body was dragged fifteen feet away from the tree; then tossed into the grave like a sack of yams.

The large, shaking hulk of Maurice Mpolo, the sports and youth minister, was led forward and placed in front of the tree. He stood expressionless, gazing toward the sky. A second squad fired, riddling the tree with holes and animating the lifeless body with gunfire, until the order to 'cesser' was given. Mpolo's corpse was then dragged tp the pit and tossed on top of the other body.

Last, Patrice Lumumba walked on one leg toward the tree, glancing impassively at the open grave. He slowly turned, carefully eyeing the four gunmen. He had a defiant sneer on his face as the last squad fired, killing the elected Prime Minister of Congo.

President Moise Tshombe took a deep breath, nodded silently at both Gat and Verschuere. He turned and walked toward his car with two cabinet ministers. They pulled away quietly along the dirt road that led back to Elisabethville.

'You must destroy them. You make them disappear,' Godfried Munongo, the Interior Minister yelled over the phone to the Commissioner of the Katanga police the next morning. Munongo was a large, expressionless, balding man, who wore tinted glasses. He was feared and carried out much of the state's dirty work for Tshombe.

'How you do it, it doesn't interest me. All I want is that it happens that they disappear. Once it is done, nobody will talk about it. Finished.'

Gerard Soete, a senior Katanga police commissioner shook his head as he listened to the orders. 'Yes, sir, we will see to it.'

'C'mon,' Soete said to his assistant, Joerd. 'We have some work to do. Some fucking awful dirty work that will haunt us forever.' They got into a police van and headed north along the highway out of town.

Soete and his assistant arrived at the gravesite under the baobab tree. He stared sickly at the site, speaking to his helper. 'Funny this tree stands for life. It's been here 4,000 years. Look at all the bullet holes. It's still standing. Let's get to work.'

Slowly, they dug up the bodies from the shallow grave. Soete took a swig from a large bottle of cheap Scotch, offering some to his helper. 'We need to dispose of these bodies. No traces. Then we'll need to fill this hole in, so no one will ever know it was used.' They began to meticulously hack the bodies into smaller pieces, each in turn, carving the hunks into even small pieces. The stench made them gag. The task and the odor made Joerd cry.

'Joerde, give me more,' said Soete pointing to the bottle. A messy pile of body parts lay on the earth before them. The job had taken nearly three hours already. 'Go get the sulphuric acid. Please,' he said with a hopeless smile. It was dark and they had more work to do.

Joerd returned with a large jerrycan and jumpily began to pour the acid on the body parts. 'Is that all we have?' asked Soete as the caked limbs hissed in the night. 'This won't do it. Oh fuck! What a fucking job! We're doing things an animal wouldn't do.'

'That's all we have,' he replied unemotionally. 'We have some petrol.'

'Come over here and sit down,' Soete said, looking out at the scene in front of him – a beautiful tree, an assortment of hissing body parts, an empty can of acid and the remnants of a half-gallon of Scotch. 'That's an order.

We will finish this,' pointing to the Scotch bottle. 'Then we will finish that,' gazing at the junkpile of mutilated body parts.

At four in the morning, Soete checked his watch. They had fallen asleep, dead drunk. The scene had not changed before him, except that there was now an empty Scotch bottle. Joerde looked up dizzy and laughed, waking Soete. 'They're still here. They haven't gone away.' They both chuckled, though their headaches and drying mouths reminded them of the uncompleted task. They rose unsteadily, both men soiled and blood caked.

'We better finish this now.' They kicked the body parts into the shallow grave. The acid had decomposed much of the flesh, though many of the bone fragments remained. 'All we can do is burn what's left.'

Joerde poured the entire contents of the ten-liter petrol can of disel fuel over the bodies. He stumbled, looking for a match in his pocket. Soete jumped in. 'I get to do this as the senior officer. Lucky me.'

A giant whoosh and an instant burst of heat and burning smoke lept into the early morning country sky. Neither of them could bear to look as the fire raged, bones crackled and the smell of diesel welcomed an otherwise beautiful mid-summer Katanga morning.

'We'll need to pick up the bullet casings once the bodies are burned. Tshombe and Munongo want a few souvenirs. Fucking animals, all of them,' said the police commissioner sas he sat in the van, waiting for the remnants of the bodies to vanish. 'How 'bout a smoke?'

Twenty-Two

February 1961

During the first week of February, President Kasavubu announced that he had named a new government to replace Mobutu's committee of commissars. Bomboko, Nendaka and Mobutu retained their posts. He also announced that Patrice Lumumba had escaped from prison in Katanga.

This wasn't an announcement that anybody believed. For the past two weeks, rumors had been circulating that Lumumba had been killed. Eyewitnesses saw him with two associates, beaten up and bloody, getting off a plane at the Luano airport in Elisabethville on January 17th, three days after his escape.

There were reports that he was tortured by the Katanga leaders and Belgian officers, forced to eat his own speeches, executed by firing squad, cut up, buried, dug up and what remained, burnt in acid. But nothing was proven.

Finally in mid-February, the story came out.

EX-CONGO PM DECLARED DEAD

According to a statement by the interior minister, 'Mr Lumumba was killed by villagers trying to take him into custody. In an official broadcast three days ago, the Katanga Government announced Mr Lumumba, 36, had escaped from Kolatey prison farm in the west of the breakaway province.'

'Well, he's a martyr now,' Denman announced after hearing that the U.N. Security Council adopted another resolution authorizing *'all appropriate measures'* to *'prevent the occurrence of civil war in the Congo, including … the use of force, if necessary, in the last resort.'* The resolution also urged *'the immediate removal of Belgian and foreign paramilitary personnel and political advisors not under U.N. control.'* The last three weeks had seen a groundswell of anti-colonialism, whipped up by the Soviet Union.

'He's getting more accomplished now than he ever did when he was alive,' Tucci added. 'Dicky, you're kind of quiet. What's up?' Penderel had been morose since the news of Lumumba's death was announced. Tucci and Denman worried about his focus.

'Look, I know how you feel about how this assassination played out,' Tucci said. 'It was going to happen. At least we didn't need to do it.'

Denman didn't respond. He was lost writing a cable to Jean-Pierre Biver, who was soon to lose his private army. *Penderel may be going through a tough time, but we can't lose sight of our goals.* This upcoming dance between the liberal U.N., a new liberal administration, and opportunistic Soviets was soon to begin. Denman wanted to control the music.

'It just didn't need to end that way,' Penderel said glumly. 'The country was coming together on its own. Slowly, and with hiccups. But allowing an assassination to go on was wrong. Flat out wrong! We say with a wink and a nod that we couldn't stop it. That's bullshit, Leon. You and I know it.'

'This was always going to be messy,' replied Tucci. 'And you knew it! Don't be sanctimonious. You've watched every move for the past year. Hell, you scripted many of them. And you did your job well.'

The camaraderie of a shared mission, so unifying at first, had frayed over the past few months. The cause that Penderel believed in was now a job he had little passion for. The people he trusted now hovered like enemies, thieves and opportunists.

He tried to remember the good times – late nights and

early mornings at the embassy trying to make this pitiful place a better place; the joys of putting information together for positive results; the drinks and laughs and toasts to successes, big and small. They seemed so inconsequential right now.

Penderel thought about why he joined Langley in the first place. The easy answer was for love of country. But the real answer was that he didn't know what else to do. He was told repeatedly that he was a hero, a national treasure to be counted on and admired. He was never that reflective. If they said it, it must be true, he reasoned.

So he continued to follow orders that allowed his conscience to bask in the glow of reflected light – shiny medals, glossy photographs, practiced looks in mirrors to present his best side. Very little had emanated from within – little self-reflection, a robot without conscience, controlled by others. Missions have beginnings, middles and endings, a linear progression of actions accomplished. Then on to the next one. There wasn't time to ask deeper questions.

Penderel spent the past year worrying about his ability to achieve what he was told to do. At first, he believed he was overrated and got in through the side door of the agency without standing in line. By the end of 1960, he had gotten that next medal, though it only came in the form of a handful of subtle compliments. That was OK, he reasoned. But the last two months had caused him to take stock of who he really was – a forty-year-old order taker, complicit in murder, who rarely questioned.

Now that Penderel had fallen in love with Beryl, he finally understood what it meant to be a real hero and a real human being. She was flawed, in some ways fatally, but she knew that life was precious, even if sometimes it ended up forgotten. He wondered about Lumumba's legacy. Would he be forgotten? A country's first elected leader. He didn't know.

Leon Tucci was packing up his briefcase to leave the mission in late-February. The uproar about the Lumumba murder still hung over the embassy, like the torrential storms that came through most afternoons. The staff spent most days fending off the foreign press about what they knew. It had become a dank, closed-in life, steamy and rotten.

Tucci overheard a conversation his boss was having on the phone. 'Well, goddamnit, go then! Hell with both of you!' was the final words he heard Denman say, before the phone slammed down. He approached his boss's halfway shut door cautiously.

'None of my business,' Tucci said, gingerly poking his head into Denman's office. Denman was smoking and studying a ream of classified documents that had come in, trying to definitively determine what happened to Patrice

Lumumba. 'But are you OK? Wanna talk?'

Denman looked up as though he was drugged and took a deep sigh. 'Troubles on the home front. Well, there would be, *if* we had a home.' He looked up at Tucci who stood in the doorway, deciding whether to go back to his desk. It was nearing 11 p.m.

'I'm here if you want to talk.'

Denman looked up, tired and relieved. 'Well, keep this between us. I'd rather my personal life not be a subject for analysis or office concern. My wife and daughter are moving back to California in May. Eliza is tired of life in London. She has no friends and wants to go home. Plus my daughter, Lola, was accepted at Berkley and wants to go to college in the States. I can't blame them.'

Denman lit another cigarette. 'We talked about the future. My wife asked if I could get a desk job doing something back home. She knows I'm not a desk guy. I told her that this is my life.'

'Is it?' asked Tucci.

'I guess it is. I'm fifty-one-years-old and I've been doing this twenty years,' Denman continued. 'I like it. I think I'm good at it too. I like the rush, the sense of accomplishing something that only I can savor. No pats on the back. No ticker tape parades. Pretty strange, I guess. I believe in my country and what it's trying to do. But this job takes everything from you and then some.'

Tucci looked up with an uncomfortable smile. 'Everything?'

'Yes, everything,' Denman continued. 'Unless you're willing to dedicate your life and risk sacrificing it, this isn't the profession for you.' He looked directly at his protégé. 'I guess I'm just like an old drug addict. I got hooked young, loved the high and now that twenty years have passed, this is who I am.'

Tucci was stunned. He never remembered Denman ever saying anything that was personal. It was all operations and planning ahead. Never looking back.

'And then, my daughter Lola started in. She called me a murderer. *A murderer!* The London tabloid press is raising all kinds of accusations that the U.S. was behind Lumumba's death. That couldn't be further from the truth. I know that, you know that. But I can't fucking tell anyone.' His voice was shaking. He was smoking his cigarette shakily, like an old man suffering from palsy.

'Oui, j'en suis conscient,' said Tucci, silently. *What kind of life is this?*

'I want to get out of here when this place calms down,' Denman said, changing the subject. 'It will soon.'

Denman was glancing at a cable that came in earlier that evening. 'Look at this. Kennedy plans to send 1,500 advisors to Vietnam. Indochina is the place to be. It's where the real cold war will be fought. Vous savez, ils parlent français aussi!' *You know they speak French there!*

Denman had regained his energy and focus. 'Both the Soviets and Red Chinese want to control that area of the world. That is *the real place* where the dominos will fall. Who gives a shit about this stupid backwater?'

'Don't forget why we are here,' said Tucci. 'Uranium. If the communists control that, then they control the domino board.'

'Perhaps, my friend, perhaps.' Denman said. Already he was onto another continent, another world, another adventure, and another fix.

Twenty-Three

March 1961

The U.N. Resolution passed in the aftermath of Lumumba's death had a minimally positive effect. A summit held in Madagascar resulted in an agreement to form a loose federal structure for the Congo. But Tshombe insisted that Katanga remain autonomous.

'Half a loaf is better than nothing,' Tucci replied when Timberlake and Denman relayed the news. 'Everyday this country inches ahead. Still, we have a constitutional crisis that must be resolved.'

Penderel knew that Tucci was right, though his heart had long since faded from the fight. Two independent states were not a viable solution. The key in this was convincing Biver and the Belgians that their long-term interest was to support a tight confederation that held Congo's June 30, 1960, borders intact. That would be a good result for the Congolese. It would halt the fighting and give this stricken, hard-luck country another chance to begin again.

'It's time to re-engage with our friends in Katanga,' Denman replied. 'Dicky, can you leave on the morning flight?'

Penderel sat on the bed, smoking. It was nearing midnight and his flight was scheduled to leave at 7. He couldn't sleep. He felt hopeless, like everything he had done for the past year-and-a-half meant nothing.

Penderel wondered if part of the problem was the Congo landscape itself. Humans come in and try to change things -- build roads, set up missions, hold elections and try to promote what the people could do together. But ultimately the physical environment swallows up any signs of progress.

In the Congo, he had witnessed what men can do to one another. At times, it seemed to be a contest to see who could display the most depravity. No one was immune. How much of it was caused by the environment around them? Was it the enormous river and the endless jungle that humankind could not control that made men wild and untamed as well? And if man exerted no control, then how can there ever be discipline or morality?

'Etienne?' Penderel called across the terminal. The Elisabethville airport was quiet and amply protected by a large contingent of Katanga troops. The Belgian military support appeared to be intact, if in the background. 'Nothing here changes,' Penderel thought, shaking his head as they left the airport.

Biver greeted Penderel as he stepped out of the elevator on the third floor. There was much to catch up on, but more not to broach. 'Glad to have you here! I'm so sorry to hear about the Cuban fiasco. Never underestimate the ability of things to go wrong.'

Penderel didn't answer. The failed *Invasión de Bahía de Cochinos* unsettled the new Kennedy administration less than three months into office. All Penderel could think was *thank God we never did anything that stupid here.*

Biver continued. 'Word has it that you've been personally invaluable in getting the Kasavubu government up and going. Or should I say the Mobutu government up and going?'

'We've provided counsel but they don't listen half the time,' Penderel answered flatly. Biver could be so damn supercilious at times.

Biver laughed. 'Yes, they're a stubborn bunch, not prone to compromise.'

'With your personal counsel and influence,' Penderel pried delicately, 'do you think Tshombe would be open to compromise for the best of this nation?'

'Stop right there, Mr. Penderel. I'm not the right person to be discussing military or political strategy.'

'Jean-Pierre, Belgian troops and other foreign military *advisors* must leave Katanga or there will be an armed reaction by the United Nations. I say this as a friend, not as a U.S. envoy.'

'I'll keep that in mind. Are you here overnight? If so, I'd love to treat you to dinner.'

'I really wish I could. I'm trying to catch up on work tonight. Been one of those kinds of weeks. I'd love a raincheck.'

Penderel returned to his room at the hotel. The meeting with Biver was frank and he relayed exactly what Denman told him to say. He liked Biver and he knew he'd do what served his company's interests best. Certainly bloodshed would not be good for business. There was not much another nice dinner would accomplish right now. Everyone had played their hand and was waiting. Tshombe was the real problem. He was a king after all.

The foreign mercenaries were another matter. There wasn't much anyone could do to expel them. They could easily move in and out of the country. Penderel had come to believe that the tedious back-and-forth negotations between Tshombe and Kasavubu were a pointless never-ending game. It didn't really matter what he did.

In the end, they would smash it like it a child's game that had no consequences. They could just choose sides and start over again. *Eeny-meeny-miny-moe*, you're on my side now. All Penderel wanted was for this country to find some modest path toward self-determination and self-discovery.

Twenty-Four

Late April 1961

Three weeks earlier, Penderel had experienced something pure and visceral that gave him energy and hope. Perhaps it was a naïve escape, he thought at the time. Everything changed, everything brightened; and the future could be great.

Penderel thought about balance in the world and seen an earlier version of man, before corruption. *What can we learn from this to understand the repressed kindness and instinctive decency we must still genetically retain?* And there was the murder of the three men he had yet to completely absorb.

The first sight of the mountain gorillas in the eerie, yet majestic Virunga Mountain range came to him – like so much of this memory – as a dream. He and Beryl had traveled for hours from Goma to reach the sleepy town of

Kisoro across the border in the Ugandan Protectorate.

The land was forbidding, with chunks of lava strewn across the silent fields, capable of only growing potatoes, maize and beans. The 14,000-foot peaks in the distance were constantly shrouded in a cold mist and fog. It was a land that belonged to the animals, the weather, the mountains, and the sky. Man had not yet arrived with AK-47s to fight over this land.

'How much further to the hotel?' asked Penderel.

'Only about a mile or so, sir,' said the driver who had picked them up at the Goma airport four hours earlier. 'The road gets rougher from here.'

They were headed for the Bwindi Impenetrable Forest. The single lane dirt road was gouged and streams regularly crossed the roadway. On their right, the mountain dropped off five hundred feet into the mist.

The Land Rover fishtailed toward the inner edge of the road and sunk into a ditch. Penderel got out to steady the vehicle and within thirty seconds, he was covered in mud. Ruddered by Penderel, the Rover slipped up the incline, until they saw the orange glow of three kerosene lanterns marking the entrance to the hotel. A tall, rugged man with two barking sheepdogs waved as the screen door slammed shut behind him in the cloudy twilight drizzle.

'The last mile is the most difficult. We're trying to raise money to fix the road,' the hotelier said, laughing in German-accented English. 'Not always a priority for the government.' He looked at the brown-caked visage of Richard Penderel trudging up the driveway. 'I see you are starting your hike early. Please come in and change. There's a fire in the stove. I'm Walter by the way.'

The main building of the Travelers Lodge hotel was comfortable, yet basic. The central area served as the public living and dining space with a small kitchen, washroom and bedroom leading off a larger room.

The proprietor was a rangy, broad-shouldered German, who had come to this region in the early 1950s. He wore a heavy hand-stitched woolen sweater and blue American dungarees. He had a large expressive face and clearly enjoyed the few visitors who came this far.

'Your rondavel is over there,' Walter said, pointing to a rounded, mud hut, roofed with thatch. 'There is a cistern in the rear. Please bring us the muddy clothes and we'll wash them tonight. They'll still be damp in the morning. You'll get used to being damp,' he said, handing Penderel a kerosene lantern.

'You're quite the explorer,' Beryl teased as Penderel stripped off his clothes and went outside to pour cold water on his body. Beryl was clean and warm, with only a few smudges of mud on her long dungarees. 'Your countryman Henry Stanley would be proud.'

'Maybe we could get into that sleeping bag before dinner?' he asked.

'I see the effects of cold weather on your body. I always thought cold water did something else to men.' She smiled at Penderel standing in the doorway, drying himself with a tiny hand towel. There was a small wooden framed bed in the room, with a lumpy mattress, shrouded in a clean white sheet. A hand-knitted woolen blanket was pulled up on top of the sheet. There was a wooden side table beside the bed.

'You know this is stupid, don't you?' Penderel asked, watching his breath in the chilly hut. 'He's going to find out.'

Beryl looked up, contentedly from the book she was reading. 'He probably knows, but he's down at the farm all week. He thinks I'm in Leo. It doesn't matter. I'm with you and you're finally going to see our greatest treasure.'

'Biver would beg to differ,' Penderel said, smiling gently. 'Never thought I'd make it here. Then again, never dreamed I'd be here with you, either.'

'Do you think your people suspect anything between us?' Beryl asked, sitting up in the small cot. 'Do you think they know that I'm your operative?'

'Oh, Denman might suspect because Denman suspects everything,' said Penderel. 'But I made it clear that I had a Belgian contact who knew things about Katanga. I already had business in Goma so he let me have a few days off,' Penderel continued. 'Anyway, I won't be missed. He's been in his own world lately.'

'He's probably down at Elysium,' cackled Beryl. 'Making plans of some sort. Dicky, you need to be careful around him. He's like Timmy – single-minded.'

'I don't think we need to worry,' Penderel said, though he worried about it all of the time. It was just that Beryl was always on his mind. He was never as happy as when he was in her presence.

Penderel and Beryl awoke to the clanging bell outside their hut. It was a little after six in the morning. 'I'm not getting out of this cocoon,' said Penderel, noticing his breath in the dim glow of the lantern. 'You can tell me later what I missed.'

'Oh yes you are, great adventurer,' she answered, unzipping the sleeping bag. 'You're going to be one of the first to see these gorgeous creatures. C'mon! It's warmer than one of those turrets you used to crawl into.'

'Maybe we can just stay here all day?' Penderel said.

'Get up, lazy ass,' Beryl answered.

Penderel nodded and got out of the bed and put on his long johns and woolen socks. 'Duty calls, I'll be back.'

'My hero,' Beryl said, watching Penderel head to the outhouse.

A little before seven, the lead guide, Wilson knocked at the door, offering coffee and warm oatmeal. The weather was damp and chilly. The clouds had closed in overnight and it was disorienting to be in an cold, alien environment with less than twenty feet of visibility.

'Today we will be lucky,' said Wilson. 'Samuel and Roland have already gone ahead. There was a family we spotted last week. They don't tend to roam too far, unless the food supply gives out.' He looked up at the sky. 'Let's hope some of this fog lifts.' Penderel noticed that Wilson had a pistol holstered by his side.

'Hope we won't need that,' said Penderel, pointing to the weapon.

'Just a precaution,' replied Wilson. 'It's rare you run into anything. Mostly chimpanzees, which can be aggressive. Maybe an odd lion. We've spotted one not far from here. They prefer the lower slopes.'

Beryl stood, stretched her hands to her feet gracefully and peered out of the hut. 'The clouds are lifting. It is going to be a gorgeous day.' She bent at the waist and touched her toes ten times.

Penderel, Beryl and the three porters followed the trail up and over the saddle. It was steep and muddy. Both Penderel and Beryl slipped as they slowly climbed through the mist and muck. The bright sun finally pierced through the canopy of bamboo and the refracted light illuminated the muddy earth below their feet.

'Your first lesson is to identify gorilla spoor,' Wilson spoke, taking a breather. They had been hiking for two hours in near silence, except for the huffing of Penderel and to a lesser extent, Beryl. 'It looks like a heel print, similar to a human foot but it's much wider,' Wilson explained, drawing the shape in the dried mud. 'Look for vines stripped of leaves,' he whispered, pointing to bamboo ahead that had been denuded. 'And also keep an eye out for holes in the ground. Gorillas love taproots.'

Wilson, Samuel and Roland pointed out remains of the gorillas' recent meals along the steep trail. Bamboo shoots seemed to be the food of choice -- both shredded and peeled like a banana. There were leaves of certain vines that were broken off and bits of wild celery were discarded along the path.

Wilson picked up several pieces of dung and examined

them. 'They've been eating some fruit. Fruit is rare up here. It's a delicacy for them. Some flowers, roots, a few slugs and snails in this too.' The climb continued.

They walked ahead and Wilson pointed to two nests in the canopy of the bamboo. They were artfully constructed of vines, bamboo and brush. 'This is where a few of them slept last night. We're getting closer.'

Samuel and Roland communicated silently yet quickly, as they walked ahead, along the trail up and over the ridgeline and down again into the narrow valley. A whistle here, a hand signal there. Their eyes darted around the suroundings, taking in every detail, piecing clues together that Penderel was baffled by. The echoing of unseen birds high above was the only other sound besides the tramping of feet and gasping of breath.

'Let's head up this way,' Samuel said softly. 'I think this is a new footprint.' Penderel looked down at the earth and saw nothing, until Samuel carefully pointed at the outline of a shape on the ground.

The group crossed a lower saddle and below sat a small group of gorillas – one silverbacked male, one black-backed male, three females, two juveniles and two infants. They were huddled and dry underneath the underhang of a rock. Six of them immediately bolted up the slope, but the large male remained behind. He was still intent on finishing the bamboo he was nibbling on. The silverback roared, startling Penderel, but Roland motioned to come closer. They were thirty yards away. He roared again.

Two females looked up, then they went back to eating. One was nursing an infant; the other was grooming one of the juveniles. The other two juveniles were wrestling, loudly grunting and barking at one another.

'Look at them,' Wilson said with amazement. He could hear deep, rumbling belches coming from the group. 'It's a sight I never tire of.'

The afternoon sun had begun to dip behind the mountains and a cool breeze rustled the leaves around the clearing. Wilson looked up and motioned for Samuel and Roland to pack up the supplies to head down the mountain to the guesthouse.

It would probably be an hour-and-a-half hike down the mountain and Penderel could already feel his knees aching. He had blisters and he was sore, but every moment of the twenty-minute sighting remained in his mind as he began the descent.

Penderel could hear Samuel and Roland a half-kilometer ahead, laughing, shouting and clapping. This was something that was much more than just a job for them and he was elated at the wonder of their shared experience.

Just then, Penderel, Wilson and Beryl heard a volley of gunshots. They were coming from below. There was loud, indistinct screaming.

'Sshh,' whispered Wilson, startled. 'Be quiet. Something is wrong ahead.'

Penderel knew the sound of an automatic machine gun. He had heard it his first day in the country. A Kalishnikov has a distinct sound -- loud, springy, and the ammo whizzed. Very different from a M4, which is sharp and popping. It sounded completely alien in the majestic quiet and calm of the Virunga Mountains.

'What is going on?' Penderel and Beryl were stunned.

'I don't know. Probably poachers,' answered Wilson. 'We need to take cover behind that tree.' The three slid off the trail into a thicket beside a huge, ancient tree. The exposed roots looked like a jail cell. 'Just be still.'

Wilson unholstered the Mauser. 'I was hoping that I'd never have to use this. Always a first time.' Wilson looked anxiously at the handgun, loading the cylinders with six .32 ACP shells.

Penderel looked over at Beryl, then at Wilson, as he fumbled with the gun. It had been a minute since he heard the shots and screams. 'Wilson, let me do that. I used to be in the military.'

Wilson looked up relieved, handing the weapon to Penderel. Penderel checked the cylinder and cocked the hammer, then released it. He took the holster from Wilson and strapped it around his waist. 'Everyone needs to be very, very quiet. Stay here. I'll be back.'

Penderel climbed unsteadily up the short muddy hill toward the trail, grabbing roots with one hand, trying to carefully to keep the gun clean. His heart was pumping from the effort and fear of what lay ahead. He began the descent, step by step. He was not trained as an infantryman.

He slowly crept along the switchback, peering over the edge. The visibility was poor. The sun had disappeared over the western brow, so the landscape was soupy and damp. He heard voices, low and garbled.

One hundred meters ahead at a turn in the trail below, three barefoot men sat on an uprooted tree trunk. One of them had an AK-47 slung across his shoulder. The two other men were arguing with him. Samuel and Roland looked to be crumpled in a heap beside the trail. The men from a distance were small, dirty and the high pitch in their voices suggested fear. They looked like wild creatures.

The man with the machine gun was lecturing the two others. They had not heard nor seen Penderel, the best he could tell. Wilson was probably right – they were poachers. But they also had the look of starving men.

Samuel's and Roland's loud and excited chatting must

have alarmed the three men and they likely got scared and killed them. Poaching was a capital offense and up here, you shot first and asked questions later. The British in charge of the Ugandan Protectorate were strict about that. Better than the damned Belgians!

Penderel took a deep breath. He didn't want to kill anybody, particularly three poor men poaching in the mountains. But he reasoned the loud guy with the AK-47 would kill them all. *He might even be in some paramilitary group. If so, they would expect others to come down the trail. Maybe that's what they were arguing about?* He couldn't be sure. Two joyful, innocent people were dead for no reason. He had to protect Wilson and Beryl.

Penderel removed the gun from the holster, aimed, took another deep breath, cocked the hammer, let the breath out and fired.

The loud report echoed up the valley as the man with the machine gun exploded before him. He turned the gun on the two others, as they screamed and pointed up the trail. They could not see Penderel as his body was still hidden in the misty underbrush. Penderel leveled his arms, breathed again and stopped.

The men got up, screeched and started to run away, leaving three dead bodies and the AK-47 behind. *Should he pursue them? No, it was getting dark. No, go get the gun*, he told himself. *That was the only thing that mattered. Then head up the trail to get Beryl and Wilson. And get the hell out of here*! He doubted Beryl and Wilson would know what had just happened. All they would have heard is the gunshot, probably assuming that he was dead.

Penderel peered out of the thicket. He had killed someone. He'd done it in the past as an occupation, but this was a real person he trained his sight on and pulled the trigger. He never thought of himself as a sniper, but that's what he really was.

But these guys had killed two young men in cold blood over nothing. Two good, young men, who could help this miserable country succeed, were dead. The two poachers who ran away were probably headed back to their camp. Maybe there were others? Everything was so uncontrollable and unknowable, particularly here.

And was this just a pack of poor hobos trying to feed themselves? Or were they killers out on patrol? It didn't really matter. Penderel felt sick to his stomach. It was time to get out of Africa. Maybe he and Beryl could just run away? To a safe, imaginary place where there was no more killing.

Twenty-Five

May 1961

Denman walked through the doors of the Le Restaurant Cedars Élevé at 1:30. He was running late, as usual. The interior was dark and smoky, particularly since his eyes had not adjusted from the bright sunshine, when he removed his sunglasses. The restaurant was half-filled.

Three tables of well-dressed Belgian women he recognized from embassy gatherings waved. There were two tables of Congolese men who looked to have nowhere to go, drinking and laughing. His counterpart from the Belgian embassy waved. He was talking to Cyrille Adoula, a respected politician who regularly attended the meetings in Binza.

He noticed his colleagues at the back of the restaurant at

a table near the kitchen, where they were unlikely to be eavesdropped on. They had already ordered a bottle of Chablis. Long afternoon, thought Denman. I've got a lot to do later.

'What's the crisis of the day?' asked Tucci, noticing Denman's preoccupation. 'Thought we had reserved today for an afternoon of drunkedness and relaxation?'

'The botched invasion in Cuba is still the hot subject. Now they'll never get Castro out. They want hearings on the Hill. Stevenson is getting pilloried at the U.N.'

'At least, it's not us,' Penderel said.

'There's a trove of conversations I'd love to be listening in on,' Denman answered. 'That's Adoula, right?'

'Yeah,' Penderel answered. 'Good guy. I'm sure Marlière is pumping him for information. Reliable. Mobutu likes him.'

Penderel had organized this lunch in the hopes of repairing an increasingly distant relationship with his boss. The Lumumba assassination still hovered, though Penderel felt sure that the U.S. had no involvement. It was a small consolation. Still, Penderel sensed that there were large holes of information that he wasn't privy to.

They talked about the future. Denman and Tucci were

likely headed to Indochina later in the year. 'If we can get Katanga settled down and a relatively-moderate, pro-Western government in charge, then that will be our legacy. Someone else will have to manage this place after us,' Denman answered. "It's been a rougher road than anyone could have imagined, but everything is on the right path forward.'

'The problem remains the mercenary army all over the east. It's not just a few colorful soldiers of fortune,' Penderel whispered. 'I hear they've got well over a thousand young white kids from all over Africa. Most are doing some god-awful things to the local population. Shooting people dead just for the hell of it.'

'Where did you hear that?' asked Denman softly. He scanned the faces around the restaurant, before continuing. 'I've heard rumors but no credible confirmation.'

'A source,' whispered Penderel, studying the other tables. They were all engrossed in their own conversations. 'Actually Habib. A lot of these Belgian military types come in here, get drunk and talk too much. He mentioned one guy from Katanga, a policeman who dug up Lumumba's remains. Pretty awful stuff.'

Denman looked up, uncomfortable. 'That's strange,' he said. 'I'd heard that Lumumba was killed trying to escape from a prison north of Elisabethville.'

Twenty-Six

June 1961

'Mr. Penderel, this is Gabriel. I work with Mr. Khouri. He has taken quite ill. He asked me to call you right away. He's at the hospital.'

'What's the matter?' Penderel asked. It was 7 a.m. Sunday morning. He had given Habib Khouri his flat number to be used only in case of emergency. Other interactions were always handled via message drops at the restaurant.

'After closing last night, Mr. Khouri got very sick. High fever. Pain in his stomach. Throwing up. His eyes were bleeding.'

'His *eyes were bleeding*? Oh, my God. I'm so sorry. Where is he?'

'At the hospital. Kintampo.'

Penderel quickly showered and got dressed. His head ached from too many brandies the prior evening. He threw on a shirt and pair of slacks. *Mr. Khouri is very sick. His eyes were bleeding.* That is so strange! He was fine when they last got together mid-week.

There was no traffic along Avenue Des Flamboyants as he left the flat. He walked a block to Avenue Prince de Liege. Not a car in sight. He crossed the roadway and jogged to Boulevard de 30 juin. A cab was parked outside a small shop.

'Il me faut un taxi tout de suite. C'est urgent. S'il vous plait, déposez-moi à l'hôpital Kintampo.' The cab driver was drinking a cup of coffee, but he quickly threw it back and motioned to head outside. They roared off along the empty street toward the hospital.

The emergency room was quiet. A good sign for a Sunday morning. So many Saturday nights, the hospital was packed with drunken young men who had been in fights. Nasty machete wounds were the most common injury. Sometimes amputations were required. Other nights the wounds would be bad enough that the bodies were guerneyed away to be sorted out in the morning.

The tribal spats were a part of the Léopoldville landscape, even when the country was at peace. Penderel asked directions and was pointed down a corridor to a waiting room. He sat down, lit a cigarette and waited for the doctor.

'Your friend is dying,' an older Belgian doctor said, as he came into the empty waiting room. 'Don't know what it is, except one hell of a virus that doesn't respond to penicillin. I've never seen this before.'

'What? My friend is dying? What do you mean?' Penderel asked.

'There are strains of viruses that get brought to the cities from inland. They can take over a body instantly. Was your friend up river or in the bush?'

'No,' Penderel said. 'He runs a restaurant. A good one. Le Restaurant Cedars Élevé. You know it?'

'Of course. Wonderful food. A very nice man. I didn't recognize him. His condition is declining rapidly. He's bleeding badly.'

'You don't know the cause? It seems so sudden.'

'Usually the symptoms of these viruses take a few weeks to appear. This is unusual to be so sudden. And all the bleeding, this quickly. It's something I've never seen before.'

'Can I see him?' asked Penderel.

'No, he is highly contagious,' the doctor answered. 'We'll need to get a list of the employees at the restaurant and recent guests as a precaution. This disease is spread by human contact. A restaurant is the worst environment for something like this.'

'Yes,' said Penderel. 'I can get you that. What else can I do? Mr. Khouri is a good friend.'

'I don't suspect he will live through the afternoon. Does he have family?'

'Yes, they are over in Brazzaville,' Penderel replied, mind a million miles away. 'I will contact them too.'

'Thank you, Mister…?'

'Penderel, Richard Penderel. I'm with the U.S. Embassy.'

'I'm Thomas De Smet. I've lived here since 1938. Something about this illness troubles me,' he said, stubbing a cigarette out in the small ashtray in the waiting room. 'Normally he would have experienced symptoms for several days, though the man who checked him in, said he worked last night and was fine. No one gets sick that quickly, unless …'

'Unless?' asked Penderel.

'Nothing. I was going to say that 'unless someone injected him with a strong dose of a virus.' But that's impossible. He'd have to be in a hospital for that to happen. Pay it no mind. Mr. Penderel.'

'Thank you, doctor. I will let you know what I find out.'

Penderel took a taxi back to his flat. Was it possible that Habib's sudden illness was caused purposely? Was someone trying to murder him? He needed to speak to Gabriel. 'Please drop me at the Le Restaurant Cedars Élevé.'

Gabriel was mopping the floor as the cooks trudged in to prep for Sunday lunch. It looked to be business as usual. 'Bonjour. Y'a-t-il des nouvelles?

'No, not yet,' Penderel lied. 'He is in isolation and the doctors are trying to diagnose what's wrong with him. I have a few questions. Can you give me the names of everyone who worked last night? And the reservation list too? You said he was feeling normal all day?'

'Yes, nothing different. You know Monsieur Khouri. He's a man of much energy. We had a busy night. Some of your friends were in, too.'

'My friends?' Penderel asked.

'Yes, yes, those two men you had dinner with two weeks ago. Americans. They were here with another man. I didn't recognize him.'

'Mr. Penderel, is Monsieur Khouri going to get well?' His expression was hopeful, but grim. He was a Congolese after all, used to bad health and bad news.

'I hope so, but I don't know. The doctor suggested I call tomorrow for an update.'

Penderel returned to his flat. He was confused and angry. He couldn't believe where his imagination was taking him. *They couldn't? They wouldn't? Why? And how? Is 'Ned from Paris' back again? No way!* Habib Khouri was a friend of the United States. And a spy for the United States! There must be another answer. He thought about others. Surely the Belgian military would have a motive if they thought he was spying on them?

He thought back to the conversation he, Tucci and Denman had over lunch a few weeks back. They were slightly loaded. Afternoon buzzes were the most fun. It had been a good afternoon to get grounded again, he remembered fondly. The first four months of the year had been hell on all of them. Three guys who practically lived together blowing some steam off. He tried to remember the conversation.

'I hear they've got well over a thousand young white kids from all over Africa. Most are doing some god-awful things to the local population. Shooting people dead just for the hell of it.'

'He mentioned one guy from Katanga, a policeman who dug up Lumumba's remains. Pretty awful stuff.'

He'd gotten that from Habib. That rumor had been floating around for months. He'd heard upwards of 25,000 disappearances, but no one really knew. That's 100 a day. A lot, but life was pretty cheap here. So much of this country was unruled and unmonitored.

And then, Denman's reaction. *'That's strange,'* he'd said. *'I'd heard that was Lumumba was killed trying to escape from a prison north of Elisabethville.'* Not one soul in the Congo believed the official explanation. Denman was probing.

Penderel called the hospital and asked for Dr. Thomas De Smet. It was nearly six p.m. He needed an update from the hospital. He dreaded making the call to Habib's wife. If the news were bad, he would take a ferry over to Brazzaville. News like that had to be delivered in person.

'Hello, Mr. Penderel.'

'Good evening Doctor. Any news on Mr. Khouri?'

'Yes,' he paused. 'He passed away an hour ago. The virus took over his entire body. I've never seen anything like it. We are performing an autopsy tomorrow. I'm so sorry for your loss.'

'Me too. I will notify his family and colleagues at the restaurant.'

Penderel sat on the edge of the bed, put his face in his hands and wept. It was his fault. He enlisted a kind, loyal and patriotic man; a far better man than he would ever be. A man, whom for the last year, had been reliable, generous and valuable to the United States. *I've gotten this man killed. I've created a widow and fatherless children. I'm stupid, naïve, and selfish.*

Penderel stepped off of the ferry and walked west along the quay towards Pogo Pogo, where Habib's family lived. He rehearsed what he planned to say, but knew something different would come out the moment he saw them. He had called the prior night when he received the news to ask if he could visit in the morning. Habib's wife was pleasant, but puzzled by the call. Why would this American be calling me and asking to visit? He didn't even know my first name!

I'll just tell her, Penderel said to himself. *I can't go into details, even if I knew them. He simply got a tropical virus. That's all I knew. That's all the doctor would tell me.*

Penderel felt sick to his stomach that he could deliver a message so cold and dishonest. *My first operative had been poisoned by his boss, for some reason. Did the loose talk about the massacres and Lumumba's death cause this?* He, Tucci and Denman had been a team for nearly eighteen months, sharing everything they knew to the benefit of this country. This was the kind of stuff they talked about all the time. It didn't make sense.

Penderel looked at the card with the address. Avenue Eduard Renard #66. It was up ahead on the right side of the road. He steeled himself as he walked up to the front door and rang the bell.

Six hundred miles away on a familiar farm on the Congo/Northern Rhodesian border, George Denman had enjoyed a relaxing afternoon, after the long flight from Leo that morning. He was tired, having been out to dinner the prior night with Tucci and Edmund Means, who worked at Langley, the man who had relayed the assassination orders to Penderel.

'You boys know how to live right,' Means said, turning to Timothy Reader, alcohol and a Kentucky accent slurring his words. 'Man, doubt it was ever this good in ol' Dixie.' Means looked out over the swath of gentle hills and acacia trees from the stone terrace. 'Man, oh man, heaven.'

Denman looked toward Reader and smiled. 'When are you finally going to turn this into a hunting retreat?'

Reader chuckled. 'Soon. As soon as things settle down around here and we can move on to more important things.'

A broad chested, tanned muscular man in a khaki shirt and shorts chimed in, 'We look forward to keeping Africa moving forward socially, politically and economically. Responsibly managing the wealth and resources of this great continent is a worthy goal.' His distinctly South African accent had an Irish lilt in its cadence and delivery.

'To my dear friends from the United States and Belgium, I'm happy to have shared a great day of hunting. The bounty of this continent is a gift to the world,' Reader said. 'Tonight, we will enjoy the fruit of our afternoon labors -- an impala. And Mr. Means, I have a taxidermist already working to prepare the Sable antelope you bagged today as a 'thank you' present for all of your efforts in our cause.'

Means stood, somewhat tipsy, but mostly tired. He gestured enthusiastically with his glass. He had been on planes for three days now and his body clock was sometime far earlier in the day. 'I'm just a country boy from Kentucky, Paris, Kentucky. Horse and bourbon country. Don't know much about Rhodesia, but I like what I've seen so far. It's been an honor to be invited here to help keep the country, I mean the Congo and Katanga, free from goddamned communists.'

Nightfall came quickly to Elysium, as Denman, Means and Hoare continued to chatter into the evening. Denman noticed the brightness of the stars in the winter sky and the clear constellations above, far from the ambient lights of civilization. This was a place chosen by the gods where the righteous and the heroic would remain to live a happy and blessed afterlife.

Later, Denman sat out on the terrace, thinking and smoking. All of the others had gone to bed, except Reader, who had stood up and moved to the edge of the terrace to look at the sky through his enormous telescope.

'This is what makes life worth living,' Reader mumbled, with his eye and body turned sideways to stare through the oculus. The Milky Way stretched above, a vibrant glowing band arched across the sky. 'There are over 200 billion stars up there. 200 billion!'

'That's a lot, Timmy,' said Denman indifferently. 'Makes us all feel inconsequential, wouldn't you say?'

'Well, somebody's certainly inconsequential now,' said

Reader. 'Too many people running their mouths is a problem we don't need. D'Aspremont and Denard recognized the Lebanese guy when we were having lunch over in Brazzaville. Assume he probably did the same. He might have put the pieces together. We couldn't afford that.'

'I agree,' said Denman. 'Mr. Khouri was very helpful, but he might have compromised the operation with his knowledge. But there still are other moving parts.'

'Who else?' asked Reader.

'Penderel has a source,' Denman answered. 'A Belgian woman who knows a lot. I've wracked my brain. How many Belgians have operational knowledge about activities in North Katanga? Or have other hypotheses on what happened to Lumumba?'

'I can't think of any,' said Reader, though his mind was already sorting through the candidates.

'Give it some thought. One other thing. Hammarskjöld means business this time. We're getting a lot of pressure to fall in line with State. Don't let this get out of hand, Timmy. The Lebanese guy is as far as we will go.'

'We're already ahead of you, George,' said Reader. 'Let's leave it at that, OK?'

'Sure, Timmy,' said Denman, wondering if a new, bigger problem was arising.

Twenty-Seven

Late June to July 1961

'So what's it gonna be George? Are you going to play ball? Or are you gonna screw me?' The new *chargé d'affaires* sat across the dining table sipping coffee. Up until that point, the initial meeting had gone well, almost too well, Denman thought to himself. James Godley, a large, gregarious twenty-year State Department veteran, had just arrived in Léopoldville to replace Ambassador Timberlake.

'Huh, what?'

'Are you going to introduce me to the Binza group? I hear they run the show?'

'Of course,' Denman said, relieved. 'Penderel's been the guy working with them. You'll like them. They are all different. Somewhere in that group, we'll find our new

Prime Minister.'

Penderel looked over at Godfrey, nodding. *I did do some good with that group*, he thought to himself. It had been a few months since Penderel had been out to Binza. Denman had taken over the primary relationship after Lumumba's death.

'They have their own priorities, for sure,' Penderel finally said, coyly.

'Now it looks like it's coming together,' Godfrey replied, looking relaxed for the first time in the week he'd been in the country. 'Who's the best option? Any ideas? You know these guys.'

'I think Justin-Marie Bomboko is the best solution,' Denman replied. 'He's competent and works well with us.'

'I agree,' said Penderel. 'But he has some baggage. His involvement in Lumumba's murder remains an issue with many of the deputies. Plus he's been a very good foreign minister.' *Everyone was involved in Lumumba's murder.*

'OK, then, who?' Godfrey asked. Godfrey liked making decisions quickly. He'd yet to realize that nothing in the Congo was really ever decided. And if it ever were, it would never be implemented.

'Cyrille Adoula,' Denman answered. 'He's been a fringe member of the Binza group. Popular with a lot of people.

Kasavubu likes him.'

'He's definitely our friend,' said Penderel.

'Well then,' Godfrey said. 'We'll need to create a little distance. Our man needs to be visibly *non-aligned* for everyone's good.'

'What if we have armed fighting in Katanga? The Soviets could affect events very easily if they wanted,' Godfrey anxiously asked his Station Chief. The new *chargé d'affaires* had not yet grasped nor accepted the topsy-turvy style of Congolese politics.

The problematic Moise Tshombe had again refused to reunite with the federation, nor expel Belgian and other foreign forces as was demanded by earlier U.N. resolutions. This only served to put the Congo back as a priority with the United Nations.

'James, I'm not so sure,' answered Denman cautiously. 'No one can steer this ship of fools. The Russians may be dumping planeloads of AK-47s up in the hills, but they can't control things any better than us.'

'But we need to be supportive of these new U.N. resolutions,' Godfrey countered. 'The elected Prime Minister of Congo was brutally murdered six months ago. People think we're behind it.'

'I think this is coming to a head, James,' Penderel said

slowly, looking at both his boss and Godfrey. 'Having it both ways is going to blow up in our faces. We cannot flagrantly dismiss a U.N. resolution. I'm sure Hammarskjöld wants this resolved by September when the General Assembly meets.'

'He does,' Godfrey answered. 'And this goddamned wall going up in Berlin is only making it worse!'

'Unintended consequences. That's all I can say,' Denman answered, sucking down the remains of another cigarette. 'Every action here results in unintended consequences.'

The stories about the mercenaries and Belgium's involvement in Lumumba's death were common knowledge. Penderel began to become paranoid about his job and the government he thought he loved. *And he had killed someone three months ago.*

After getting the bodies down the mountain, Penderel called Denman to explain what happened. Denman didn't care. *You had to do what you had to do*, he said, coldly. *That man would have killed you too.* Penderel had left out the details about who his travelling companion was, though he assumed a story like that would have gotten around the white ex-pat world of central and eastern Africa. It had been reckless to travel like that with Beryl.

Penderel increasingly thought about Beryl. She was the one person who was trustworthy and anchored. And he had done something heroic, worthy of her admiration. He had saved her life.

He and Beryl had experienced something together that very few human beings had before. His host at the Travelers Rest had said something about the mountain gorillas that stuck with Penderel. *There is magic, humanity, love and gracefulness that will disappear before our grandchildren will get to see them.*

Having experienced magic, humanity, love and gracefulness with Beryl, Penderel felt that whatever came after that point of no return was all right with him.

Twenty-Eight

August 1961

'Would you come over here and hug me, please?'

Beryl leaned back naked on the pillows on the bed in his apartment. She had just taken a sip of champagne that Penderel fixed for her. She noticed the reflection of her open legs in the mirror. Today, she didn't feel strong or confident. She looked up at her saggy breasts and disheveled hair and felt cheap. Penderel was in the bathroom.

'What's that?' he yelled over the running water in the sink.

'I want to you to come over here and hold me *tightly.*' She watched her expressions in the mirror and enjoyed seeing her lips move as she uttered her demand. Her makeup was smudged.

'Just a minute,' Penderel said as he entered the room, drying his face with a small white towel. 'You seem upset. Everything OK?'

'No, *everything isn't OK*. Can I have a cigarette?'

'Sure.'

'Do you think I'm pretty?' she asked, lighting the cigarette and taking a long deep drag. She turned her head as she gazed into the mirror.

'Yes, you know that I do,' answered Penderel. 'I've found you stunning ever since I first laid eyes on you on that flight to Elisabethville.'

'I think you are a beautiful man,' she said smiling. 'You've saved my life and I love being with you.'

'Me too,' Penderel said quickly, starting to button his shirt. Beryl lay in bed, unguarded, naked, warily watching him, smoking.

'People told me I was beautiful when I was a young woman,' she answered. 'Of course, you never really know that yourself.'

He looked over at her as he zipped up his pants and

began to put on his necktie. She was smoking another cigarette, blowing concentric smoke rings toward the ceiling, then slowly she turned her head, watching the light on her countenance change. It was as though her image in the mirror was all that she had left. 'I think he knows about us. Something he said a few days ago. A wisecrack.'

'What?' Penderel said, sitting down in the ratty chair with the fraying fabric with the bright, oversized cabbage rose pattern.

'It was an argument. He's pretty dug-in about Katangan independence. It was something he said about 'driving all the U.N. and American sympathizers out of here.' Then he said, 'Maybe that's something you can help with?' It was the way he looked at me. Or maybe the way I reacted?'

'Maybe? But Beryl, I wouldn't overreact. Your husband has a temper and can be mecurial. We all know that.'

'Dicky, I'm worried that these guys don't know when to stop. There are people my husband works with who are radical. They'll do anything to protect what they think is theirs. Tshombe is just as corrupt as they are.'

'Do you want us to protect you? It's always been out there as an option. Or I have a better suggestion. Why don't we just go away together and start a new life? We have to get out of here. I love you, Beryl Reader.'

Beryl looked up, joyous. A sudden flush of happiness came onto her face. Five seconds later it was gone. "No, I was born an African, and will die as an African. You know they will find us wherever we go. I'm sure about that. We are doomed people. Both betrayers. We will meet in the afterlife. At Elysium.'

Twenty-Nine

Late August 1961

'It's nice to finally see the Belgians pulling their troops out,' Tucci said, reading the cable that just came through.

'There are still 20,000 of them left, though,' answered Penderel. 'All working for the UMHK.'

'Isn't that good?' Tucci answered, trying to judge Penderel's bitterness.

'It would be if they weren't siphoning so much money back to Belgium,' Penderel answered. 'They're not going anywhere. Just think, the money could be helping to protect the wildlife here.'

'Oh please! When did you get to be such a bleeding heart?' A conservationist?' Tucci asked. 'I agree that this place is completely rancid, but all of this is good for American interests. Get over it.'

'Leon, I get it. I really do. But I'm worried about my operative.'

'Yes, the one you we didn't need to even put on the payroll. That's quite the accomplishment!'

'Screw you, asshole. I haven't heard from her in two weeks. I'm worried. She thought that her husband had found out.'

'Why don't you try your friend Rene? He might have picked up some chatter from the Belgians in Katanga. The Belgians aren't that cautious. You just have to listen harder.'

'Good idea. Anything to get some answers.' Penderel was lost in his own world, guilty about his recklessness with Beryl.

'Be careful,' said Tucci warmly. 'Rene's a good guy, but we don't always share the same goals. This whole stance on Katanga is tricky. He's a friend, until he's not our friend.'

Delvaux and Penderel sat at a table in the rear corner of the Zoo restaurant. They had selected a nice bottle of

Bordeaux and the Nile perch for dinner, but first were enjoying Black Labels on the rocks. There had been a shortage of good Scotch lately, so they were both glad to savor the healthy slug that Fabianne poured when they walked in.

'What's today's crisis, my friend?' Delvaux asked. 'You don't look like your jovial self. Perhaps a Sunday outing to the club to perk you up?'

'That would be very nice. Thank you. The crisis is the usual one. How to get Tshombe back into the union? The U.N. is finally going to put their money where their mouth is.'

'Yes, I've heard,' said Delvaux, relaxed, legs coiled around each other. 'Or rather the U.S. is putting your money where the U.N. mouth is. We're pulling our troops out. You've probably read that.'

'Yeah, but there are plenty still around. And I hear lots of trigger-happy boys out to make some money killing Congolese. '

'Advisors to the government and military. You know damn well that Katanga has been the one thing we can all count on. Tshombe's stubborn, but consistent. I'll take consistency any day over corruption. Corruption will always be there. Yes, there are pockets of some young white Africans. They are on someone else's payroll, thankfully. '

'Tell me,' Penderel asked leaning in. 'Or don't, if you can't. What do you know about Timothy Reader? A friend of Biver's.'

'*Friend* might be too strong a term. He's just an advisor. He's not under our umbrella, thank God. Tshombe pays him.'

'What do you mean?'

'He's one of the crazies. There're a number of militant white Africans wanting to keep Katanga as their playground and piggy bank. Tshombe's their figurehead. They're not to be crossed. You didn't hear it from me, but he was involved in Lumumba's murder.'

'I'd heard that,' Penderel replied. Beryl had all but said the same thing. 'So where does Reader fit in?'

'Tshombe's paying him, but Reader's group wants Katanga, South Africa and Rhodesia to be its own white-run country. Seriously. They run the mines and the railways. The white Africans have got this twisted notion about the land. They have been on it for a century and are not leaving.'

Delvaux sat back along the banquette sipping a brandy, watching Penderel absorb the information. 'It's pretty frightening, even for the UMHK crowd. All they want is business as usual.'

The restaurant was quiet for a Wednesday, even though it was nearing 11 p.m. 'Just anything you can find out about him, his wife, his contacts. You know, the usual stuff,' requested Penderel, stunned at the revelation.

'I'll see what I can find out. I guess I shouldn't ask about your relationship with him?'

'No, probably not.'

'See you on Sunday. Noon OK?'

Thirty

Early September 1961

Delvaux had assumed his usual wolfish perch by the pool at the Funa Club. The more things changed in Leo, the less the club did. It was still an oasis outside the city where he spent his Sundays, trying to pick up European married women. Since independence, the club had decided to admit blacks, although there were very few that Delvaux noticed. It was expensive to join.

There were three young white men sitting poolside, drinking and playing cards. Rene guessed that they were South African mercenaries by the broadness of their accents and the leathery tone of their skin. These weren't political advisors or spies.

'I joined up for the money and to get away from my

wife,' one was saying. 'And if she doesn't improve as a housekeeper and a mother for our kid, I'll sign up for another six months.'

They all laughed and shouted for another round. Delvaux smiled and looked at his watch. 'These guys will be blotto by noon.' He sat back in his chair and listened. Penderel should be here by now, he thought.

'I came for the money and the adventure," said a tall, attractive broad-shouldered blond boy, who looked to be around twenty. He guessed that he was Kenyan. He was loud and didn't seem to care that foreign mercenaries were expelled from this country. 'I used to travel with a magician's vaudeville act up until I turned eighteen.'

'Now you are a man of principles,' said the father figure desiring a better homemaker. He looked to be no more than twenty-five.

'A man of principles? Fuck no! Put it this way. If Jomo Kenyatta wanted volunteers, I wouldn't join up. I like Tshombe. He's the only white African left. Who's paying for this round?'

A muscular, dark-haired guy removed his hat and sunglasses. 'I will. My turn. Ah, those lovely American dollars,' he said, fingering a roll of $100 bills more than a quarter-inch thick.

Just then Penderel walked up. He looked relaxed, wearing a pair of oatmeal colored linen pants and an open collared navy polo shirt. 'What have we here?'

'Some tourists on vacation it appears,' Delvaux said. 'Good to see some white people back and supporting the Congolese economy. Can I get you a drink to help you enjoy the show? Quite a group!'

'Sounds as though you've been here awhile too.'

'Three Lillets. I promise to behave this afternoon. Maybe they know your friend Timothy Reader?'

'Any word?'

'Yes,' he said slowly. 'You're a busy man, my friend.'

Penderel's heart sank, as he took a short sip from his small glass of Jupiler. Delvaux smiled as he continued to watch his expression. They had been playing this game for eighteen months now. Who would be most careless? Whose mouth would twitch? Who could get the better of whom? It was about to be clear.

'Your rendezvous were noticed. We did first. Then Tshombe wanted you watched. No one knows where she is. She vanished into thin air driving back from the university. Some word that she was depressed. Might have done herself in. That's what's being floated. Nothing confirmed, but her husband knew she was giving you information. We knew you were fucking her, but that's not a crime. I'm sorry you're in this mess. Reader is vindicative as hell. You need to be really careful.'

Penderel sat at the table motionless, lighting another cigarette. *Oh my God! What have I done? I've gotten someone else killed. She wanted to help, to build a better Congo for everyone. She just wanted love. She just wanted love.*

He thought back to their last meeting. *I was born an African, I will die an African. We are doomed people. Both betrayers. We will meet in the afterlife. At Elysium.'*

Just then a fourth young guy joined the table alongside the pool. He was thin, wearing swimming trunks with a large jeweled crucifix around his neck.

'Are you religious?' the Kenyan asked. 'That's quite a cross to bear.' He laughed at his own pun.

'Not particularly.'

'Why the crucifix?'

'Oh that. I took it from a Baluba who no longer needed it,' he answered. 'He came at me from about fifteen yards with a Mauser. I fired at his head. It was hard to miss. In a manner of speaking, you might say I ventilated his think box.'

'I knew this one South African called Frenchie,' the young father said. 'I'd say he enjoys the killing. I'll bet he's killed 300 blacks himself. They'll be driving by a settlement and just opens up with a machine gun from the armored car. I've seen him laughing. Sick fucker.'

He continued, ordering another round. 'There were four of us drinking beer in a hotel room in Stanleyville about three months ago when he heard a loud thump overhead. Some guy, must have been a sniper, had fallen through the cheap asbestos roof. We could hear him running along the ceiling. We followed him, listening to the *thump, thump*, room to room, until we got him. Dumb ass fell through the ceiling, dead as a rock with six holes in him.'

'Waste not, want not. Six slugs for one guy?' the Kenyan asked. 'We're trained to be more efficient.'

'We carried him out of the hotel lobby, dumped him in the brush, returned to the room, washed the blood off our hands and cracked another Tusker. Nobody said a fuckin' word.'

They all started laughing again. Another round was ordered.

Quiet had come over the table next door. The loud, running description had sickened Penderel and Delvaux.

They were middle-aged men, not young mercenaries, yet they were working for organizations that were these guys' paymasters.

'It's an odd business we're in,' Delvaux continued, quietly. 'I look at those boys and think we're doing the same goddamned thing. We're just management.'

'People like that killed Lumumba and probably Beryl too. Shot them, burned them in acid, spread what was left out over the landscape. Africa is a big, unforgiving place,' Penderel said, voice shaking.

'Indeed, my friend, indeed. Any interest in tennis today?' Rene Delvaux understood the moral ambiguity of what he did. Best not to linger on it too long. His children would never need to come to Africa. His son would go into the family beer business after university. His daughter would be married in five years. And he'd be retired within ten years.

'No,' said Penderel. 'I'm feeling tired. A few more Jupilers and a club sandwich is all I can manage. Sorry.'

'No problem,' Delvaux answered. 'I'm sorry about this. None of what we do is very clear-cut. The two sides are not good and evil. That is the problem with these proxy wars. Because we aren't doing the shooting, it's easy to see it as a bloodless contest. For us it's about stopping the Soviets. But the Congolese are the ones dying.'

'You need to be *really* careful, my friend. I mean this sincerely. Everyone you wished *not to know, knew* about you and Beryl. She was practically wearing a neon sign around Leo when she visited. She's one weird lady, but one of the few with moral fiber. Not a particularly delicate operative.'

'I feel like such a fool.'

'You're not a fool. Idealistic, naïve, maybe. Horny, definitely. This business is not for idealists. That's what happened to Beryl Reader. She wanted to believe. But deep down she knew she was on a suicide mission. She understood the stakes of betraying her people. She believed in the possibility of what Africans could do for themselves. She was a progressive lady. Maybe deluded, but I always admired her.'

'She always talked about her soul remaining in Africa,' Penderel said. 'That it would return to Elysium. Now it all kind of makes sense. I'm a stupid man.'

'No, just a latter life idealist,' Delvaux smiled, tossing back the last of the Lillet, with a wink toward Penderel.

'I need to find out for sure,' Penderel moaned. 'I've fallen in love with her.'

Delvaux stared over at Penderel silently, before he began to speak gently. 'She was an exceptional woman who had a rage to live and deserved love. But you need to grieve privately, or you too will be killed. I suspect you've next up on the crazies' hit list. I'm not sure who you can trust.'

'Oddly,' Penderel answered. 'Just you.'

Thirty-One

Mid September 1961

'George, do you have a minute or two?' Penderel asked, knocking on Denman's door. He didn't trust his boss, but he knew that he had to discuss Beryl's disappearance with Denman and reveal their relationship. And maybe Penderel could find out something.

'Come in,' said Denman.

'As you know, my operative disappeared last month,' Penderel began. 'It was Beryl Reader.'

Denman looked up, genuinely surprised. 'I knew you were having an affair with her, but never in a million years, thought she would betray her cause. That whole group of people we've gotten to know in Katanga is driven, maybe even mad, but incorruptible.'

'Incorruptible?' Penderel asked angrily. 'They are pure evil. Only focused on their goal of a white Africa. Beryl couldn't stand that. So she came to us. Said the United States was the only hope for this country.'

'They are quite focused on retaining the status quo,' Denman answered. 'And they have very different perspectives on how that should be done.'

'I think Reader killed his wife, just like he killed Lumumba,' Penderel blurted out. 'Murdered her, chopped her up and burned her remains. I have no proof. Will you help me get it? He's probably after me next.'

Denman sat back in his chair, rocking like a metronome. Seconds passed, until he spoke. 'No, we can't. We are not in the business of settling scores. She knew the risks of beginning a relationship with you … and us.'

'Don't we take care of our operatives?' Penderel pleaded. 'Hell, I still haven't got a satisfactory answer to what happened to Habib Khouri. Someone poisoned him. That was not just a garden variety virus he contracted.'

'I can't comment on Mr. Khouri,' Denman answered. 'I suspect some people thought he knew too much.'

'But that's the goddamned point, George!' Penderel screamed. 'His intel was about the Belgians' role in knocking off Lumumba. Hell, someone even approached me last year about assassinating Lumumba with poisoned toothpaste. I thought it was a joke.'

Denman continued rocking back and forth. 'Yes, we knew that. And you handled it appropriately. Lumumba was for the Congolese people to sort out. And they did.'

'With a few white helpers,' Penderel said.

'George, I can't take this anymore,' Penderel continued. 'I'm burned out. I can't sleep. I can't even see straight anymore. I want to go home. This job is not for me. I can't do it.'

Denman leaned forward in his chair, nibbling on the inside of his lip. He exhaled loudly. 'Dicky, this job takes your soul away. It grinds you up and leaves you in little pieces that don't fit together. I understand what you are saying and I'll help. I'll begin the process with Langley. You've been a great asset to the agency. I didn't think so at first, but you've proven me wrong.'

Penderel sat back in the small wooden chair, stunned. He never expected George Denman to react the way he did, much less compliment him.

'Let's get through this Hammarskjöld visit later this week,' Denman said. 'These next few days are going to be hell. Trying to get him comfortable with what's going on and get him to bash Adoula's and Tshombe's heads together. What a week ahead!'

On September 12th, Secretary-General Hammarskjöld left New York to fly to Léopoldville. The General

Assembly meeting was scheduled for the following week and the Secretary-General looked forward to providing a first-hand report on the progress toward reconciliation. He also had been working to broker a face-to-face meeting between Adoula and Tshombe.

Penderel had met Dag Hammarskjöld once, though he'd spent a good deal of time the last two months reading what he had to say. Hammarskjöld seemed to be the only person involved in the Congo who had a shred of balance and compassion for handling the problem. Every one else had taken a stance at the poles of the self-interest spectrum and was going to fight to the death. There was serenity and hope in Hammarskjöld's writings that made Penderel believe in the power of human dignity and mutual respect.

Dag Hammarskjöld had dominated post-war diplomacy, taking the U.N. from a sidelined organization, beholden to Cold War dynamics, to the one accepted and vital international problem-solving body. He was known to be both an earnest Christian philosopher and a secular practical man of action. He was respected for his ability to bob and weave through the competing interests of the Permanent Five and was fond of quoting Martin Buber, the Jewish prophet -- 'the only reply to distrust is candor.'

'Mr. Godfrey,' Hammarskjöld began quietly, but firmly, just after arriving at the U.N. Mission in Leo. 'I will personally meet with President Tshombe to discuss Katanga's reintegration into the country. I believe that I am the only one who can persuade him to travel to

Léopoldville to meet with Prime Minister Adoula. I have relayed this message to him. We will leave for Ndola tonight.'

Godfrey and Denman talked in the back of the car as they returned to the U.S. Embassy. They both admired that Hammarskjöld was willing to put his reputation on the line to negotiate with Tshombe. They had no illusions that Tshombe would budge in his stance. He was playing the long game, after all.

'We should be at that meeting,' Denman remarked.

'I've never met Tshombe,' said Godfrey. 'Plus having a U.S. State Department official there will piss the Russians off. They'll say that this is an international problem to be solved by the one unbiased body in the world.'

'Why don't we send Penderel?' Denman suggested. 'He knows Tshombe. Knows the dynamics in Katanga. He even has a few contacts in Elisabethville. He's just a consulate officer, so no red flags.'

'He's the war hero, right? The one who'd rather fly missions than kiss Marilyn Monroe?'

'Yeah, he's the one. Good, hard-working agent,' Denman replied. 'He's provided a lot of useful info. He's had a tough few months. Two of his operatives were killed. Not sure he is long-term agency material. But this is the perfect occasion to get him back into the flow of things.'

'Well, let's brief him when we get back. I already feel

better knowing we'll have ears on the ground.'

Denman just looked ahead, uncertain of how Tshombe and his crazy foreign white allies would react to a visit from the Secretary-General. *Tshombe will agree to a meeting with Adoula. Then he'll renege. Hammarskjöld will push for a larger U.N. military presence in Katanga. The foreign interests will get nervous with the world scrutiny.*

He was pretty certain of that. The last thing Reader and his white African friends wanted was scrutiny.

'How far would they go?' Denman wondered. *Are they crazy enough stop reconciliation? All Tshombe wants is to control Katanga and the mines. But he already has that with a foreign proxy company and private army. He'll entertain the fanciful thinking of Reader's crazy friends wanting to establish a white-run nation. He'll still be king.*

But what worries me is that none of these people give one shit that the visitor is the Secretary-General of the United Nations. But would they do something really stupid? Perhaps? Then all hell would break loose. The world would know about everything, particularly that nearly pure strategic rock deep underneath their soil that could destroy the planet a thousand times over.

Denman had watched this series of events and contingency plans spiral out of control and he feared the worse. But having Penderel in the meeting provided comfort and continuity. If the meeting goes well, we'll know and get full credit from the U.N. If the meeting goes poorly, he thought, *well, we gave it our best try*. He rang Penderel at the embassy.

'You're going with Hammarskjöld tonight to Ndola. Go get your suitcase packed. We'll brief you as we head out to the airport. No one should know you're going.'

At 1751 hours, a chartered DC-6B registered as SE-BDY and known to its crew as the *Albertina* took off from N'djili airport, Léopoldville, for Ndola.

Penderel sat in the third row of the plane, behind Hammarskjöld. He had never taken this flight privately, nor had he flown in darkness above the Congo before. It made him feel important again. *I'm in the center of the action for the first time in months. Denman's not a bad man after all.*

Penderel laughed as he dogeared a page in the book and closed his eyes. *The Agony and the Ecstasy* sat on his lap. This has been like painting the Sistine Chapel! He hoped the payback from the agonies of the past year would come. This was the perfect opportunity. Tshombe would have to give ground this time. The whole world was watching.

'I'm a fan of your writings,' Penderel gently said, after unbuckling his seat belt, standing up, and approaching the Secretary-General. He had wanted to speak with Hammarskjöld before they arrived at Ndola. They had been flying for nearly five hours. The night air had been smooth.

Hammarskjöld looked up with a wry twinkle. He too had been reading a book. The New Testament. *A man on a whole different wavelength. This guy really is a saint!* Penderel thought to himself.

'Thank you,' Hammarskjöld replied. 'I've kept a diary my whole life. Sometimes a few entries get published in the papers.' He spoke perfect, barely-accented English. The sleeves on his pressed white shirt were freshly ironed and he had not loosened his navy tie. He was formal and elegant in appearance, but his blue eyes were bright and welcoming. His brownish-blond hair was longer than Penderel expected, yet it was neatly combed back.

'Freedom from fear' could be said to sum up the whole philosophy of human rights.' That was something you wrote a few years back,' Penderel recited proudly, concerned that he might be overdoing it. But here was the most important man on the earth, the only person who could bring this civil war to an end.

Hammarskjöld grinned modestly. 'Did I say that? I probably borrowed it from Martin Buber. He's far more articulate and thoughtful than me.'

'I believe this will be a good meeting,' Penderel answered. 'I know Mr. Tshombe and believe he will be receptive to your entreaties for peace and reconciliation. He too is a spiritual person.'

'Yes, Moise is an alternative spelling of Moses, but I'm not sure how driven by spirituality he is,' Hammarskjöld nodded with a wink. 'I expect he will drive a hard bargain.' Hammarskjöld's quiet confidence and bright eyes intimidated Penderel. 'But it is critical that Katanga unify with the remainder of the country.'

'You are probably the only one he will listen to,' said Penderel. Penderel smiled, nodded his head, turned around and walked back to his seat, as the plane began its initial approach into Ndola. But he was not remotelty sure that Tshombe would give one inch of ground, even to the Secretary-General of the United Nations.

'I hope you are right, Mr. Penderel,' Hammarskjöld shouted over the load, humming propellers.

At 2335 the aircraft called Ndola with the estimate that it would be abeam the airport at 2347 and would arrive at 0022. At 2357, the *Albertina* requested clearance to descend.

At 0010 the aircraft radioed 'Your lights in sight, overhead Ndola, descending, confirm QNH.'

'Roger QNH 1021mb, report reaching 6,000 feet,' answered Ndola.

SE-BDY replied 'Roger 1021.'

Penderel looked out of the plane window over the moonless, black landscape. For nearly six hours, he had not seen another light on the ground until now. It reminded him of how enormous the country was. Their plane was just a speck flying over miles of emptiness below. It was like those night missions over Europe and Korea, so many years ago. But this aircraft was roomy and comfortable and the flight had been smooth.

They would be landing soon, according to the pilot on the PA system. The small tower at the airport was off in the distance, its beacon circulating. Peace was at hand.

Penderel suddenly heard the sound of another aircraft, though he couldn't tell where it was. He guessed it was flying above. The sound was familiar. It was an engine he'd heard before.

The *Albertina* turned toward the starboard as it began its approach. Just then, the smaller plane came alongside. 'This asshole's flying wing-to-wing,' remarked Penderel under his breath, as a muffled rumble arose from the anxious passengers looking out of the tiny portholes. 'It's that fucking Fouga.'

Bang-Bang-Bang. Ping, Ping, Ping, Whoosh. Three shotgun sounds hit the wing and fuselage of the *Albertina*, lacerating the DC-6B. A bright explosion lightened up the dark sky. Penderel looked around the small cabin as the plane began to rock, side-to-side. He had experienced this sensation before.

The plane's two right propeller blades had been hit and one of the fuel tanks was on fire. Panicked gasping filled the plane as it lost altitude. Penderel's mind flashed to the scene seven years ago over the Yellow Sea. This time no one had a parachute or an ejection seat.

The pilot tried to keep the plane steady as it began its freefall. The propeller blade had penetrated the lower fuselage of the aircraft, severing the electrical wiring for the propeller controls and some engine instruments. The g-force and shrill sound of a falling mass from the sky was the last thing Richard Penderel remembered, before he blacked out.

The shattered, melted fuselage was resting on a large termite hill, nine miles from the airport in rough bushland, when the official inquiry team reached the crash site fourteen hours later. They identified one survivor, Sergeant Harold Julian, who had a fractured right ankle, skull injuries and burns over more than 50 percent of his body. All of the other passengers were dead. Sergeant Julian would die five days later.

The body of Secretary-General Dag Hammarskjöld was lying peacefully thirty yards away. He was on his back, leaning against a termite hill, immaculately dressed in pressed pants and a white shirt with cuff links. One of the rescue team commented that he looked to be taking a short nap after a vigorous walk.

His left hand was clutching some small leaves. His nearby briefcase contained a copy of the New Testament, a

German edition of the poems of Rainer Maria Rilke, and a copy of Martin Buber's *I and Thou.* A copy of several American newspaper cartoons mocking him and a scrap of paper with the first verse of Gene Vincent's 'Be-Bop-a-Lula' were folded in his wallet.

The mangled body of Richard Penderel was found inside the fuselage. The contents of his briefcase were never revealed, though a folded article from the *Stars and Stripes* and a copy of Irving Stone's *The Agony and the Ecstasy* were found beside him in the wreckage.

Epilogue

Fifty-three-and-a-half years later, there is still no definitive answer to what happened on the night of September 18, 1961, when the *Albertina* crashed in Ndola in the Federation of Rhodesia and Nyasaland, presently known as Zambia. There have been numerous official inquiries and several published accounts, yet nothing has ever been conclusively proven.

Beside U.N. Secretary-General Dag Hammarskjöld, there were sixteen passengers on board who were killed, including the Swedish flight crew, members of his staff, an armed security team and one American, identified as Richard Penderel, a consul to the U.S. Embassy in Léopoldville.

Local residents reported that a second plane, a Fouga Magister, attacked the DC-6B. One man recalled that he had seen the same aircraft landing many times over the past several years at a nearby airstrip. The sole survivor of the crash said the plane 'blew up' before it went down. The wreckage was reportedly found and sealed off by Northern Rhodesian troops and police at dawn, though the official report said the plane was not discovered until three the next afternoon.

Officially it was ruled an accident due to pilot error, though later inquiries suggested the cause of the crash would always remain a mystery.

In December 2014, the Swedish government requested that another inquiry be reopened to determine the cause of the crash. There was reportedly evidence, bolstered by Charles Southall, a former U.S. naval officer who was working at a National Security Agency listening post in Cyprus on the night of the crash, that the Central Intelligence Agency has a tape-recorded radio communication by a mercenary who carried out the alleged air attack on Mr. Hammarskjöld's plane.

On March 16, 2015, *The New York Times* reported that the United Nations had appointed an independent panel to assess the 'probative value' of evidence that has surfaced in the decades since the last formal inquiry. The three panelists – Tanzanian jurist Mohammed Chande Othman, Australian aviation expert Kerryn Macauley, and Danish ballistics specialist Henrik Larsen will be empowered to travel to the scene of the crash, interview eyewitnesses and draw on documents that the United Nations has urged its members to disclose. Their report is due in three months.

Secretary-General Dag Hammarskjöld was posthumously awarded a Nobel Peace Prize in 1961. President Kennedy called him 'the greatest statesman of our century.' He was buried in Uppsala, Sweden, three months after his fifty-sixth birthday.

Richard Penderel was given full military honors and buried at Arlington National Cemetery. He left no survivors. He was forty-one-years old. Records about his service for the United States after the Korean War remain sealed.

George Denman left his position as Chief of Station, Congo in 1964 and went on to a twenty-five-year-career in the CIA, including postings in Southeast Asia. He died in 2008 in Virginia at the age of 86.

Leon Tucci had a twenty-year career in the CIA, followed by a successful diplomatic, political and business career. He retired in 1995 and resides in surburban Washington, D.C.

Joseph Mobutu became President of the Republic of Congo in 1965 (renamed Zaire in 1971) and served until 1997 when he was overthrown and expelled. He died in Morocco three months later of prostate cancer.

Clare 'Tim' Timberlake, the first U.S. Ambassador to the Republic of Congo from 1960-1961, later held senior State Department and Arms Control and Disarmament Agency positions until 1970. He died in Maryland in 1982.

Moise Tshombe was President of the secessionist province of Katanga between 1960-1961 and later Prime Minister of Congo between 1964-1965. He reportedly died of heart failure in 1967, after his plane was hijacked to Algeria. He was fifty years old.

Joseph Kasavubu was the first President of the Republic of Congo, a position he held from 1960-1965. He died at age 59 at his farm in Boma, in far west Congo on March 24, 1969.

Justin-Marie Bomboko was an active Congolese politician, serving as foreign minister three times (1960-1963, 1965-1969 and again in 1981.) He died in 2014 at age 85 in Brussels after a long illness.

Victor Nendaka was the first head of the Security Services in Congo from 1960-65. He later became Minister of Interior and the Ambassador to West Germany. He died in Brussels in 2002 at the age of 79.

Cyrille Adoula was the Prime Minister of the Republic of Congo from 1961-1964. He later served as Ambassador to the United States and Belgium, before retiring from politics in 1970. He died in Lausanne, Switzerland in 1978 at age 57.

Prescott Dillon went on to become Deputy Director of the CIA, until his retirement in 1975. He died in Chevy Chase, Maryland in 2005 at age 90.

Jean-Pierre Biver was Chairman of the Union Minière du Haut Katanga (UMHK) from 1955-1963. He died the following year of cancer at age 58.

Count Harold d'Aspremont Lynden, Belgium's Minister of African Affairs from 1960-1961, died of unknown causes in 1967 at the age of 53. Posthumously, he has been accused in many accounts as being the central character in the planning of Patrice Lumumba's murder.

Beryl Reader disappeared on August 19th, 1961, on her way home from work at the University of Elisabethville. Her body was never found.

Timothy Reader died of a gunshot wound to the head in November 1961 at a farm outside of Elisabethville. No one was ever charged in the shooting, although there were rumors that the CIA was involved. There also were unproven allegations that he was involved in both the assassination of Patrice Lumumba and *Albertina* plane crash.

Rene Delvaux retired from the Belgian security service in 1970 and lived with his family in Leuven, Belgium, teaching at the University until 1983, when he died at age 73.

In 1997, Zaire was renamed the Democratic Republic of the Congo. Today, the crisis in the Congo continues and it remains a dangerously unstable country. Over the past two decades, there have been an estimated 5,400,000 deaths as result of the continuing civil war in the country, making it the world's deadliest conflict since World War II. The international plundering of its abundant natural resources, wildlife and minerals continues unabated.

Acknowledgements

First, I want to thank Heidi, my wife of nearly thirty years, for her support and encouragement throughout the process of writing this book. She made terrific suggestions along the way that improved the flow of the narrative and character development.

I want to thank a group of friends who provided terrific counsel over the past six months. These include Parke Muth, Fred Hitz, Ned Carter, Sally Suthon, Annie Izard and Sally Neil who pushed me forward, reined me in and provided great insights into the plot, characters and historical detail. I want to thank Porter Scott for his valuable help with the French translations. Merci! I also want to thank Barb Wallace – again – for all of her help and talent on the cover jacket design. All of these collective suggestions, critiques and inputs reinforce the notion that it takes a small village to help one person to write a book.

Last, I want to thank Ross Howell, a friend and Adjunct Assistant Professor of English and Creative

Writing at Elon University for his fine editorial assistance throughout the entire process. He has been a godsend to me as a new, later life writer, determined to improve with each effort.

This is a work of historical fiction, so the narrative follows a timeline of actual events that occurred in this eighteen-month period. In addition to the *Foreign Affairs* article that piqued my initial interest in the remarkable story, two prior works of non-fiction were critical in better understanding the time and events of the period. These included Larry Devlin's 'Chief of Station' and Madeline Kalb's 'The Congo Cables.' Both had tremendous and insightful perspectives on this fascinating, but largely unknown time in world history.

In addition, there are scattered and innumerable accounts of this crisis in the Congo that I was able to read, digest and recreate. God bless the Internet!

About the Author

James Bell is an author who lives in Charlottesville, Virginia with his wife of 29 years and two daughters. His three prior novels, 'The Screen Door: A Story of Love, Letters and Travel', 'The Twenty-Year Chafe' and 'Christchurch' attracted a loyal following among a tiny audience of family, friends and a few strangers.

This is James' first work of historical fiction.

Made in the USA
Lexington, KY
23 March 2015